Dedication:

To my fellow authors in the Realms of Lurin:
Thank you for making this series with me.

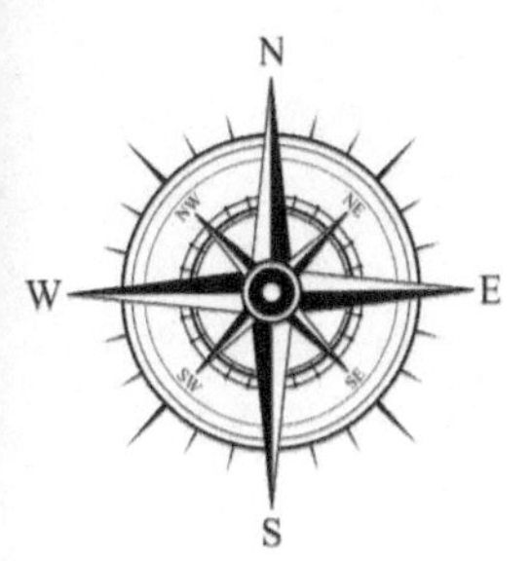

N
NW NE
W E
SW SE
S
LURIN
THORNVEIL ISLE
AKININIA
NEBRARIA
BOER
LUMIARA MOUNTAINS
ROSEMERE
OCEANEA
EKLOS
SANDOVAL

Chapter One
The Heartbreak

Lenora held her breath, waiting and watching. Her heart beat so furiously that she thought it might burst. She clutched at her chest, peering through her bedroom window to study the finely crafted horse-drawn carriages, pulling through the curving path, leading to her family's manor and well-manicured front gardens.

She should be joining the party downstairs, a party intended to find her and all the other eligible maidens of Oceanea suitors, but she wanted to have a chance to study Thomas before he could spot her.

Lines of gentlemen and ladies had already come and gone. There was a lull in arrivals, and Lenora worried he might not even attend the ball.

Her stomach tightened at the thought.

Perhaps it was better if he missed tonight's event, but her treacherous heart reached for him anyway. She told herself she'd wait for three more visitors to arrive before forcing herself to join in the reverie that floated up from downstairs. She began to sweat as the warm sun beamed through her window, where she kept her forehead pressed against the glass.

Eight carriages later, she didn't trust herself to blink, worried she might've somehow already missed him.

Thomas stepped out of his carriage, and a sound, halfway between a sigh and a sob, escaped her trembling lips.

"Thomas," she whispered, reaching her cold, numb fingers toward her window. Thomas's hair glistened in the setting sun, looking almost copper instead of its normal golden hue. He was as handsome as ever, more so even. He donned a new navy-colored waistcoat and jacket that complemented his pale skin and hair. Lenora knew it had been purchased for just this occasion – she had been with him when he sent the order to the tailor.

Hot tears cascaded down her cheeks.

They'd shared their first kiss that day, and she had pictured herself dancing with him and running her hands along the smooth lapels. He rarely allowed himself such indulgences as new clothing, even with his father's newly acquired wealth. But Thomas had claimed nothing else would do for him to announce his betrothal to Lenora.

Thomas bowed, extending a hand back inside the open carriage. Lenora held her breath, anticipating what came next.

Elisabeth Wendleboom stepped out, and Lenora's heart sank. The Wendlebooms were old wealth, much like Lenora's family. Mr. Wendleboom was a family friend and a trusted council member of the Sea Farers, a group charged with the protection of Lurin's southern coast.

Elisabeth's pale golden hair contrasted with Lenora's dark ebony. She considered whether this was what Thomas preferred about her or if it was Elisabeth's soft-spoken nature. Although Elisabeth and Lenora had played together frequently as children, she wasn't sure what the girl thought about anything. Elisabeth was one of those women that seemed to have no real feelings of her own, and Lenora, try as she might, didn't envy this about her former friend.

Lenora's face crumpled as the handsome couple smiled at each other before being led out of view by her family's butler. Gasping, she pulled herself from her window and muffled her cries with a handkerchief. Her chin quivered as she sank to the floor.

She was a foolish girl of seventeen. She should've known better than to fall for Thomas McKraven's charms. There were rumors of his less than gentleman-like behavior, courting several girls last season at one time, but he had assured her that was in the past, and Lenora was the love that he had been waiting for.

Well, she hoped Elisabeth would have better luck.

Or do I?

She squeezed her knees hard against her chest, wanting to disappear.

Yet part of her yearned for Thomas, wishing he would grab her for a dance, or better yet, apologize profusely and ask her father for her hand.

Her breathing was shallow and ragged, but if she didn't get a hold of herself soon, her lady's maid, Hettie, would probably drag her to the ball.

Why was this happening?

She closed her eyes and prayed. No words came to her overwrought mind except please.

Please. Please. Please.

She repeated it over and over until she thought she'd go mad.

If the Maker was in control, why hadn't He given her her heart's desire? She'd never wanted anything as much as she wanted Thomas. Didn't she deserve happiness as much as Elisabeth Wendleboom?

It wasn't fair.

Elisabeth grew up with doting parents, whereas Lenora grew up with a distant, distracted father, whose responsibilities kept him otherwise occupied.

Sniffling, she dragged herself along the floor to the small glass tank that held her pet axolotl. Axolotls were rare underwater salamanders – an unusual gift from her late mother that she hardly remembered. She wasn't sure how long salamanders normally lived, but she was thankful he was still with her eleven years later, even if her mother wasn't.

His pale, delicate pinkish skin and feathery, frilly external gills glided through the water, making her feel a sliver of peace.

"Hi there, Loxi."

Axolotls' mouths were drawn in a permanent smile on their small, round faces, but she could almost imagine that she saw it widen whenever she spoke to him.

Loxi swam in a circle, and her lips twitched for a moment before they fell. "I bet you're glad you don't have to worry about getting married."

A knock sounded at her door. She tensed. Her lady's maid, Hettie, was here to drag her downstairs, and how could she blame her? This was Lenora's party. She needed to show her loyalty to her father and feign interest in one of the many suitors her father approved for her.

"One minute!" Her voice sounded warbled and was barely audible. She cleared it several times before trying again. "I-I need a few more minutes."

"Lenora," her father's gruff voice spoke through the door.

She jumped. What did he want with her? Was he upset she wasn't already downstairs?

Wiping at her tear-stained cheeks, she glanced in her gilded mirror and let out an airy breath. Her skin was red and blotchy, and she had a circle on her forehead where she'd left it pressed against her window pane. She hadn't expected Father. They'd once been close, but over the last year she'd barely seen him. Worries over the pirates and sea monsters had him busy in meetings, while she was consumed with the marriage market.

Or had pretended to be.

Even though she'd accepted other suitors' visits, she hadn't considered any of them other than Thomas.

"I'd like to speak with you. Most of the guests have already arrived."

She cracked her door. "I'm still getting ready."

Her father sighed.

"Father?"

The silence of the moment continued, and Lenora opened the door another inch to confirm her father hadn't left. His brow was furrowed, and shadows circled his kind eyes.

"Father, is everything alright?"

He shook his head, kissing her blotchy cheek. He squeezed her hands, not meeting her eyes. "I'll see you at the ball."

She nodded, watching him walk down the long hallway that led to the central staircase of the house before clicking the door closed behind herself. She leaned against the door, and let out a deep breath. *What was troubling Father?* Did he notice she'd been crying? Or was he worried over his business with the Sea Farers?

She chewed her bottom lip. Rumors had spread amongst the women about the ocean's monsters getting more aggressive, even attacking as close as the shoreline, but surely Father would've told her if they were in any real danger.

Her heart sped up at the thought. She hadn't seen the ocean in years – since before her mother had died of a strange and sudden illness. She closed her eyes, trying to picture her, but whenever she did, she'd see her mother stretched out, weak in her bed, instead of splashing on the beach, where she had been happiest.

The sky outside Lenora's window had gone from orange to a darkening shade of blue-gray as dusk turned to night. She sighed.

She was now very late to her own party – well, Lord Darlington's. As the lord charged with the protection of Lurin's southern coastline and the father of an eligible daughter, he was expected to host at least one of the season's opulent balls.

Lenora splashed water on her face from the basin her lady's maid had brought in earlier, before she grabbed her elbow-length silk gloves. Her fingers trembled, making it a difficult task.

Why had Father come to see her? The worry in his eyes formed a hard knot in her stomach. Her mirror confirmed she had gone from blotchy to pale. She wished she had thought to procure some rouge for tonight's event. A lady could get away with just a little if she was subtle enough with it. Slapping at her cheeks for color, she plastered a smile on her face before forcing her hands into the gloves.

If her father was troubled, the best she could do would be to support him by not embarrassing him in his own home. The music and the din of conversation from the party floated up to the second story of their manor. She paused at the top of the stairwell, waiting for a footman to notice and announce her. She forced her gaze forward, staring out over the chandelier of sea glass and shells that hung above the foyer and front hall of the house.

She kept her chin high, flicking her fan open to cool herself on the hot summer night.

She would not look for Thomas and Elisabeth.

She would enjoy her party, dance with suitors, and move on. She had to.

Chapter Two
The Ball

"Miss Darlington," the footman announced.

Lenora kept her head high, forcing her gaze not to search out Thomas and Elisabeth amongst the crowd of guests. She wore a new dress, a pale blue empire-waisted muslin – perfect for the heat – patterned in elaborate beading that caught the light. A navy silk ribbon tied at her waist with coordinating feathers styled into her chignon. Her hair had a few loose curls, framing her pale face, matching the elegance of her gown.

Lenora had picked the navy accents to match Thomas's new coat, to signify they were a couple. This carefully planned detail only further added to the pain of the moment. Surely there were other similar shades amongst the party goers, and her foolishness would go unnoticed.

White stars rushed across her vision as she descended the long, spiraling staircase.

Maker, why have you abandoned me?

Her prayer offered her no comfort and sent her pulse racing. She shouldn't have reminded herself of how alone she was in this world.

How little anyone cared for her.

Breathe, she ordered herself, as she ran her hand along the highly-polished banister leading to the ground floor. *Breathe.*

A small crowd of eligible men gathered at the base of the stairs. *Be flattered*, she told herself, but the attention felt shallow. Hollow.

None of them knew her, not really. They liked the power her father held, and the position in society they'd be granted with a Darlington as a wife.

She smiled at them, but inside where her heart should be was a cavernous wreckage – completely hollowed and echoing the name *Thomas*.

She had been herself with Thomas, shared her hopes and dreams – traveling all of Lurin – getting to experience all the magic and wonder their world had to offer instead of being stuck inside an Oceanean manor for the rest of her days.

Word of fae, goblins, dragons, and all manner of creatures existed beyond her country's borders. How could one be content with a normal life, knowing such magic existed only hundreds of miles away?

Thomas seemed to mirror her ambition, but had it only been a manipulation for her affections?

Obviously, it had.

She held in a sob. She was a fool.

If he'd been after a title, he would've asked for her hand. The fact that he'd chosen Miss Wendleboom showed he held true affection for Lenora's soft-spoken childhood friend. The Wendlebooms had come to ruin and would have little to offer for a dowry.

Murmurs of conversation flooded around her. Her grief gave way to a hot, seething anger that burned away every kind and gentle thought she'd ever held. She wanted to find Elisabeth and throw a cup of punch in her face.

"Miss Darlington," one of the men bowed, extending his hand. "May I have this dance?"

Gritting her teeth, she bobbed a curtsy, accepting his hand as he led them to the dance floor. Golden vases stuffed with colorful feathers and blooms of flowers were spaced between the large open windows. Refreshment tables along the walls were crowded with delicacies, including seafood, which was rare and expensive now that most fishermen feared the ocean. Father had obviously spared no expense preparing for tonight. It pained Lenora to know he'd gone through such efforts to make this day special.

The violins and harp struck up a celebratory tune that had everyone smiling, except Lenora. Couples crowded the dance floor. Lenora allowed herself to be pulled along in resigned acquiescence.

"Miss Darlington, how are you enjoying the summer?" asked her dance partner. She realized at that moment she didn't remember his name.

Robert? Richard?

"It's been hot." She forced a laugh, relying on muscle memory to guide her through the steps of the dance as she inventoried her suitors' names.

Maybe she'd have a chance to overhear someone talking to her dance partner, so she'd be saved from the embarrassment of admitting her blunder. He'd called on her several afternoons this summer, once even offering her a bouquet, but she couldn't remember his name nor any personal information about him or his family. As an eligible maiden, she should've done a better job of attending to such details.

But try as she might, the only suitor she'd focused on had been Thomas. She had every one of his calling cards from his visits tucked away in her pillowcase. The rest had been tossed in with the rubbish.

As Lenora danced, the beaded patterns of her gown caught the light, creating waves of color. She spun and turned again as she was passed to another partner, letting her skirts twirl. If she could make herself focus on the dance, then maybe she could force herself not to hunt for Thomas.

But of course, he was dancing too. Smiling broadly and laughing gaily, like he hadn't betrayed her and broken her heart mere weeks ago.

She quaked as he drew nearer and nearer. She had to bite her tongue to keep from calling out to him, from running to him.

Her heart swelled as she was passed off to him.

Thomas.

His smile faltered for a second as his eyes landed on Lenora. He guided her through the dance steps, looking past her. She stared up at him, silently begging him to reconsider.

But he didn't glance at her once.

"Thomas," she whispered.

He kept his chin high, pretending he hadn't heard. It was the worst kind of punishment. Her heart squeezed as she tried to catch his gaze. Unwelcome tears pricked at the corners of her eyes.

"Thomas," she whispered again, louder this time.

But he pretended not to hear, keeping his eyes away from hers and transferring her along to the next gentleman.

Lenora took the change in song as an opportunity to excuse herself from the dance floor and distance herself from Thomas.

She settled near an open window, hoping the night air would help cool her flushed skin better than her fan, but there was barely a breeze.

A group of gentlemen with their backs to her began arguing. She recognized Mr. McKraven, Thomas's father, among them.

"I don't care what kind of deal ol' Darlington thinks he's made with those pirates. We should evacuate the coast!" McKraven spoke in a gruff tone that made Lenora jump.

"How can anyone negotiate with those rebels? Has he forgotten the war?"

"Who cares about that, McKraven? Do you really think we should leave our homes?"

McKraven snapped, "And get away from the sea monsters? Yes, I do. Last week, the Smiths nearly had their estate washed away."

"They shouldn't have settled so close to the shore."

"The Smiths are hardly the closest anyone's ever built a home – there used to be dozens right along the water. You're too young to remember. Eventually, we'll be pushed as far as the forests or the mountains beyond Oceanea, and now no one can sail either."

"The pirates do –"

"'*The pirates,*' he says; Fearless, blood-thirsty killers they are."

Lenora knew that the men hadn't noticed her, or else they would hold their tongues. Talk of pirates, the sea monsters, and the attacks were not discussed in front of women, and certainly not Lord Darlington's only daughter. Her heart sped up. She'd known there were increased concerns and that the attacks had gotten worse, but to hear these men question her father's wisdom so openly frightened her more than the rumors.

If Father didn't know how to protect Oceanea, who could?

Lenora adjusted her gloves and smoothed her skirts, fidgety with anxiety. Did her father know families were considering abandoning the country? Would her father praise her for the knowledge she'd overheard, or would he scold her for hearing it? As a woman, she shouldn't be involved in such a conversation, but she also feared discovery if she moved. Wanting to avoid scandal, she tucked herself deeper into the window frame, hoping the open curtains would block her from view if one of the men looked in her direction.

"Mark my words, Lord Darlington's got something big planned."

Thomas's father was the first to walk away, and the group slowly dispersed amongst the other party guests. She let out a heavy breath, and the gallop of her pulse slowed.

As soon as she walked toward the center of the party, several more gentlemen, including the one from before, asked her for a dance. Dizzy and breathless from the heat of the crowd and the argument she'd overheard, Lenora opened her mouth to request a cup of punch when the clinking of glass stole her attention.

Chapter Three
The Announcement

Lenora's father pushed toward the edge of the dance floor as the last song ended, tapping a silver spoon against a flute of champagne.

"My daughter and I are pleased to have you all in our home this evening." His words toned an anxious edge, sending a new swarm of butterflies through her.

A surprised murmur greeted his speech.

Father looked exhausted and a bit disheveled. Lenora's brows raised as he continued. "I apologize for interrupting the festivities, but I have an announcement to make…" He yanked at his collar like it was too tight. If anything, he looked worse than when he'd checked on her mere hours ago, like he'd swallowed a toad.

Lenora gasped. *He wouldn't…* Could her father have come to an arrangement with one of her suitors? She couldn't imagine any other reason her reserved father would put himself front and center like this.

He cleared his throat and continued, "I would like to announce my daughter's betrothal."

Lenora swayed as every eye turned toward her. Is this what he had come to her room to discuss earlier?

She chanced a glance in Thomas's direction. He leaned close to Elisabeth, not even appearing the least bit interested, stinging every fiber of her heart.

She scanned the party, but the men who all caught her eye seemed as bewildered as she. Who could her father have chosen?

Enough time had eclipsed that the hushed silence transformed to a din of confused gossip. Lenora swallowed, flushing from the stolen glances thrown her direction.

The front doors to the estate were thrown open with a bang. Gasps greeted the outburst, shushing the crowd again.

But Lenora's father, instead of investigating the interruption or appearing startled, hung his head.

A chilling silence followed as a towering man with a scruffy beard, long dark hair, and sun-weathered skin pushed his way to the center of the room. He wore a fine suit and polished boots, but it couldn't disguise him for what he really was – a pirate.

A pirate. Lenora leaned against a pillar to keep from collapsing. Many of the women fainted, others began to fan themselves with more vigor.

"Have I missed it?" the pirate asked in a low, gruff voice.

Her mouth hung open. Father knew this man? Had he invited him to the ball? She thought of the conversation she'd overheard. *"I don't care what kind of deal ol' Darlington thinks he's made with those pirates."*

Several of the gentlemen in attendance stepped forward with crossed arms, looking ready for a brawl, but if Lenora's father invited this man here, there must be a good reason.

"No," Father answered. "You're just in time." He turned, meeting Lenora's gaze. "As I was saying, I'd like you all to raise your glasses and congratulate my daughter Lenora and Captain Devonshire."

Lenora blinked. *What?* The room spun, and her heart thrummed as the murmur of disquiet roared through the party guests. Stars flooded past her vision – she couldn't take in a full breath of air.

Surely, she hadn't heard that right, *Captain Devonshire.*

Lenora knew every eligible family in the southern region of Lurin, and she didn't know a single Devonshire. Even though the pirate stood next to her father, she searched for someone, *anyone* else.

To her horror, her father crossed the length of the ballroom, looping his arm through hers, and led her to the center of the room.

To the pirate.

Women shrieked around her, and Lenora froze, unable to speak or react. Her father patted her hand, mumbling something indiscernible.

She was mere feet away from the rugged stranger when her father let go, hurrying away. The pirate wouldn't look up. She stood there in a daze, watching as her father pushed through the crowded ballroom.

How could he do this?

She leaned away from the captain, fully clutching the closest pillar and trying to catch her father's eyes, but he was making work by exiting the room, dodging several other men, no doubt trying to get a reasonable explanation out of him.

The area around the stranger and Lenora cleared, as the town's hunched, white-haired minister shuffled to the center of the room.

"N-no," Lenora croaked. "No."

Captain Devonshire looked at her then, reaching for her hand, his brown eyes blazing with intensity. His face was impossible to read, expressionless, and a bit stern. "I know this must be a great shock to you. I had wanted to meet with you privately, but your father insisted this party was the perfect place for a formal announcement. We've been planning this for years, but I can tell this is a complete… surprise." He frowned as he said the last word.

Years?

She trembled. Captain Devonshire dropped her hand, and it went immediately to her mouth. She couldn't think. Couldn't speak.

She covered her lips with a trembling hand, letting out a warbled yelp.

The minister cleared his throat, shifting on his feet. "We are gathered here today…"

The captain lifted one of his jet black eyebrows, taking in her reaction. His skin was bronzed, but his clothing was as fine as the rest of the gentlemen in attendance.

"I don't…" She began, feeling light-headed. Swaying, Lenora fell into the captain's arms. He politely steadied her again.

Lenora moaned.

"Perhaps we could wait until later?" the captain asked the minister.

Her eyes flickered to his, hope blooming in her chest.

The minister frowned. "Lord Darlington was clear that the betrothal ceremony must take place at once."

Instead of arguing further, Devonshire glanced at Lenora's wide eyes and wobbling chin.

The minister cleared his throat. "We are gathered here today in the presence of the Maker…"

Every dream she'd had of her future came crashing around her. She'd never heard of anyone being married off to a pirate, nor a betrothal ceremony coming mere minutes after an announcement. She wrung her hands, staring off into the distance. Her father had disappeared. Her guests stared in open dismay as the minister rattled on in an unenthused monotone.

Why would Father do this?

The pirate reached his hand out, revealing two shiny pearl earrings. They were beautiful, but she didn't want them. She didn't want to be engaged to this strange man.

The minister grabbed one, jabbing it through her left ear before Lenora could react. She stepped back with a cry, suddenly brought back to the current moment.

"N-no!" she shouted.

The minister leaned toward her, attempting to pierce her other ear, but she stepped away.

She'd been led to the pirate and the minister like an animal to slaughter, but she could fight this engagement. Her eyes widened as she spun, searching for a way to escape.

The crowd of her party guests pressed in a tight circle around them. Could she break through the crowd and end the ceremony? What would Father say? What would the other families of Oceanea do? Her body quaked. Her friends and neighbors offered her no help nor an escape route.

Devonshire stepped forward, blocking her from the minister. "Don't touch her again. It can wait."

Lenora's heart squeezed at the unexpected ally.

The old man sputtered, "I'm doing my job."

She relaxed for a moment, and the minister took the opportunity from her brief distraction to jam the other earring through her remaining ear.

Devonshire snapped at the man. "I told you to wait!"

But it was too late.

A small squeak escaped her lips, and she collapsed to the ground.

Chapter Four
The Escape

Lenora awoke in her room with a cool rag resting across her forehead. Her lady's maid, Hettie, sat next to her bedside.

"How're you feeling, Miss?"

"What happened?"

"I was told you fainted during the engagement ceremony."

Her hands flew to her throbbing ears, touching the smooth surface of the pearls. "Am I promised to that pirate now?" Lenora whispered.

"Yes, Miss. To Captain Devonshire. I've been instructed to pack your belongings. I-I wish I could come with you."

"No… no. We aren't wed yet… Why am I leaving?"

Hettie wiped at a stray tear, and Lenora sucked in a breath. Hettie's sorrow confirmed her worst fears.

"Your fiancé is a captain, and he sails in the morning."

Lenora's stomach plummeted. She was going to traverse the dangerous southern waters? None of this made any sense. Why would her protective father, one of Oceanea's Sea Farers, send her out to the ocean?

Hettie patted her hand. "I heard it was a lovely ceremony," she cajoled, sounding utterly unconvinced by her own words.

"I'd hoped it was a nightmare." Lenora gave a broken laugh. "If I fainted during the ceremony, it can't be binding, right? I didn't agree to anything." Acid filled her mouth as she thought of marrying this stranger – of having to press her mouth to his sun-weathered lips.

Hettie said nothing.

"Well? What do you think? Is there a way out of this? If I speak to Father…"

Lenora searched Hettie's eyes, but the maid glanced away before answering, "No, Miss. I'm afraid I've been told you are Captain Devonshire's intended. Your father has left, but he gave me this letter for you."

The maid pulled a sealed envelope from the folds of her skirt as she stood. "I'm so sorry." She wrung her hands. "It's been a pleasure serving you these last seventeen years. If it wasn't for my family, I'd come with you. I'll give you some time alone and come back in a few hours to help pack. I've been instructed to tell you your ship leaves at dawn."

As Hettie clicked the door shut behind herself, Lenora heard the maid break into sobbing.

Lenora closed her eyes, willing herself to wake up from the nightmare.

Once Hettie moved further down the hallway, the nighttime sounds of cicadas filtered in Lenora's open windows.

"Your ship leaves at dawn."

Tears rolled down her face. Father hardly let her leave the manor without a team of escorts and only for the season's parties. Never anywhere near the water or shore since her mother had passed. Most children were at least allowed to play in the sand and the shallows, but not Lenora.

He was sending her out with a stranger into the monster-infested waters he'd kept her from all these years. Her head ached, and her throat and eyes burned from crying, but she couldn't stop herself.

Nothing made sense.

The last two years of her life had been focused on parties, gowns, and the marriage market. Why had her father let her entertain suitors if he had planned her future?

She rolled to her side, watching Loxi swim dizzying circles in his tank.

She sat up on the edge of her bed.

There had to be a way out of this arrangement.

Swallowing the bile rising in her throat, she determined to fight it. She'd heard rumors of broken engagements before; they were rare, but they did happen.

The afternoon she had spent staring out her window, searching for a glimpse of Thomas, felt like a lifetime ago.

Her heart slowed to a normal rate, and she could think clearer. Since her father had fled, she had no way to plead her case before her ship embarked. Why did she need to go with her fiancé at all? What impropriety! How dare her father do this to her and flee like a coward!

If her mother was still alive, maybe Lenora would've had a voice of reason to turn to, but she had no one and nothing.

The Maker had abandoned her.

She couldn't very well refuse her betrothal. Who would marry her? Every eligible bachelor who had been thrilled to dance with her tonight would not go against her father's wishes and enter into the scandal of pursuing a promised woman.

She screamed as she clenched and unclenched her fists, slamming them against her feathered bed. When that was no longer satisfying, she threw her pillow and bedding into a heap on the floor. She yanked at her curtains until they tore from their rods. Unsatisfied, she lifted her heavy wooden chair, crashing it against the mirror. The glass shattered, much like her heart.

Exhausted from her brief display of defiance, she sank to the floor like a ship yanked down into the deep by a sea monster. She cried at the helplessness of her situation, cried for her dreams, and cried for her lost love, Thomas, which felt shallow in light of her current situation.

Loxi floated in his tank, a fixed smile on his pale face as his gills moved in the water. She placed her palm on the cool surface of the glass, and the amphibian bumped his nose against it, as if offering condolences. She knew he was just an animal, incapable of understanding, but it was enough to break her from her despair.

She pressed her face against Loxi's tank as she formulated a plan.

If she missed the ship in the morning, would the pirate stay behind and search for her? She bit her lip. It seemed too easy a solution to work, but she started to pack a few belongings: a change of clothing, her hair brush, and some kind of jar for Loxi… She couldn't bear to leave him behind. Perhaps she could sneak down into the kitchen and grab some provisions, but the real question was, where would she go? She could hop aboard another ship headed anywhere, but as she overheard last night, the townsmen were no longer risking the churning ocean waters, so another ship would likely be another set of pirates.

She shuddered.

She could start walking north. If she went when it was still dark, she might evade detection and get far enough away from the people who knew her… but how could she provide for herself? She paced her room. She didn't know a thing about hunting, foraging, or gardening, and she hadn't been allowed near the shore in years to take up fishing. What could a young maid of seventeen do to provide for herself in 18th-century Lurin?

She remembered her father's note then and found it tucked amongst the pile of blankets. She cracked the wax seal.

Lenora,

No doubt you are confused with my decision, but please know that I love you. I send you into Captain Devonshire's capable hands, believing he can keep you safe where I cannot, and grant you the freedom you no doubt long for.

Love,
Father

She wrung her hands, crumpling the note.

If he loved her so, how could he crush every one of her dreams? How was sending her out to sea, laden with monsters, a place she could be kept safe?

It was rumored pirates had their methods against the creatures, but she doubted she'd be safer than tucked away inland. The only part of the letter that rang true was regarding her freedom. She felt much like her pet axolotl, stuck in a cage on display. She'd hoped her future marriage would allow her more freedom, maybe even travel, though a pirate ship was hardly what she would've pictured.

Closing her eyes, she imagined herself by the open sea, the wind in her face and the blue water stretching endlessly. She didn't hate it…

A knock at her door sounded – she'd run out of time.

Hettie cracked open the door, taking in the view of the trashed room and rucksack, half-packed with belongings. "Looks like you've already started. I'll have the men bring you up a sizable trunk instead of this satchel." She overturned the bag, smoothing out the dress Lenora had hurriedly shoved inside it.

"Hettie…"

"Don't mind me, Miss." The old woman squeezed her fingers, before neatly folding the frock and grabbing a wardrobe-full more.

"Hettie, will I need this many gowns at sea?"

"I won't have you looking like a peasant, whoever you're married to!"

Lenora sank back onto her stripped bed, watching every one of her belongings, besides her furniture, stuffed away. In the end, her pet axolotl was carried downstairs in his full-size tank. Hettie remade Lenora's bed and tucked her in for the night, like she did when Lenora was little, planting a kiss on her forehead.

Chapter Five
The Ship

Lenora had been woken and dressed on time, but no one had allotted space for tearful goodbyes. Every servant of their large manor wanted to see her off. Hettie clutched her, sobbing into her shoulder.

Lenora gripped her lady's maid tighter. Growing up without her mother, Hettie had filled the role of a maternal caregiver.

The carriage driver cleared his throat for the fourth time.

Hettie cupped her face. "I know the Maker has great things in store for you, Lenora."

Lenora nodded, not liking how final the words sounded. She hugged Hettie again until the driver snapped at the pair of them. "Ladies, I can only push the horses so fast. We need to leave. Now!"

Hettie kissed her tear-stained cheeks and helped her into the carriage seat. The footman handed her Loxi's tank, and then they were off.

Lenora stared out her carriage window, watching the sun begin its ascent as her family home became a speck in the distance, twisting at her overwrought heart. She hugged

Loxi's tank on her lap, not trusting it to be safe anywhere else on the bumpy trip.

The carriage raced, almost ejecting her from her seat several times – the driver hadn't been exaggerating about pushing the horses.

She couldn't believe Father had left without a goodbye. She clenched her teeth and squeezed Loxi's tank with renewed intensity. What made her angriest of all was she hadn't had a chance to confront him for his decision. She couldn't believe the man who had loved and protected her her whole life had sent her into the arms of a pirate. There had to be something she didn't understand.

Ugh!

She kicked at the carriage. His note had only filled her with more questions. Yesterday, when her father had come to see her, he'd seemed unwell and worried. What kind of life awaited her on Devonshire's ship?

The other Sea Farers spoke of the sea monsters' increased aggression and her father's deal with the pirates. The dangers explained her father's absence over the last year, but maybe there was something more to it than that.

Maybe he had been ashamed to face her.

Was this engagement the aforementioned "deal" with the pirates? Devonshire had said they'd been arranging it for years. Years.

A wave of dizziness made her sway until the sloshing of Loxi's tank brought her back to the present moment.

What did a pirate want with a wife?

She trembled with nerves. Her half-eaten breakfast churned in her stomach. Devonshire had seemed kind, protective even. She clung to this bit of information like a life preserver thrown into the deep.

Despite her many, many concerns, yearning filled her, and it was hard to sit still, even with a glass tank of water on her lap.

She'd always loved the ocean and had fond memories of it from her early years. After Mother had died, Father became more protective, and she'd been barred from anywhere near the shore. But when Lenora closed her eyes, she had faint memories of the sand and waves, of laughing and splashing and her mother's smile.

She opened her eyes, staring out her carriage window again, eagerly awaiting the first glimpse of the ocean. Even with its dangers, the memory of the wide open water filled her with longing and hope.

A shimmering line of blue started on the horizon, catching the light and growing larger. Lenora couldn't picture anything more beautiful, as hard as she tried. She breathed in the salty air with reverie.

The carriage jolted to a stop, and she got her first glimpse of her new home.

The massive ship was nothing like the weather-beaten vessel she had pictured. It could house hundreds, maybe thousands. The wood beamed in the sun, like finely polished mahogany, and the unmarred white sails, a beacon of promise, billowed on towering masts. The shore was a din of activity. Men carried parcels off and on the boarding plank.

Her footman and driver carried her heavy trunk together up the narrow gangplank and onto the ship, and then returned for Loxi and his tank. Hovering right outside her carriage door, she watched with detached interest. Even though she was here, she couldn't picture her life aboard this ship.

Eventually, the crew untied the ropes, helping hold the ship in place.

Her heart sped up, and she turned in a circle. No one came for her. In fact, not a single sailor glanced in her direction. Her heart pounded.

She asked the footman, "Are you sure this is the right ship?"

"Yes." He bowed, taking his place back with the driver.

The carriage driver snapped the reins and started away. Her throat tightened, watching them leave. She would've thought they'd stay and see her off, not abandon her like this.

Where was Captain Devonshire?

She turned back toward the ship in time to see the pirates pulling the gangplank from shore. She ran toward it. "Wait!"

The men released it, allowing her to step upon it. It had seemed plenty sturdy and wide from the shore, but as she shuffled over the open water, she swayed. Her pulse thrummed in her ears, and her stomach clenched, threatening a reappearance of her meager breakfast.

Forcing her gaze ahead, she put one foot in front of the other. She took slow and steady breaths and made it halfway across. Her confidence rose until a sudden gust of wind caught her full skirts.

She dropped, clutching the wooden beam.

The sailors paid her no mind, offering no concern nor criticism of her predicament.

When the wind died down, she pushed herself up on her trembling legs and hurried the rest of the way to the ship. Stepping onto the deck, she exhaled the breath she'd been holding, collapsing on the spot.

The sailors raised the sails and shooed her out of the way to pull in the walkway, but no one spoke to her or even acknowledged her. Lenora hadn't been sure of what to expect, but she thought the captain would've gone to some effort to see her safely aboard. He had seemed concerned for her during the engagement ceremony. Perhaps she shouldn't expect gentleman-like behavior from a pirate.

There had been no other ships in the harbor, but there were many other harbors along Oceanea's coast. A tight lump of fear settled in her chest. If she was on the wrong ship, surely someone would have told her? How did she know the footman hadn't been mistaken? Her pulse roared in her ears.

It was too late to turn back now.

Lenora clung to the side of the ship as the sails snapped in the wind, drawn to their full height, pulling her away from everything and everyone she had ever known and into the vast ocean.

The lurch and sway along the waves made her light-headed and nauseous, but she couldn't take her eyes off her country. The coast was bereft of homes, due to the sea monsters, but it was the land she had grown up on – the only land she'd ever known. Her mind flashed to playing on the shore. Laughter and warmth filled her mind. Could she find happiness here? It seemed impossible.

She blinked back tears as her childhood grew smaller on the horizon. Her heart squeezed in her chest, longing for her home with Father. When she'd pictured moving out, she'd assumed it would be for love and after an extravagant wedding. Her dreams crashed around her in time with the jostling ship. She sobbed, watching the land disappear into the ocean until there was only blue in every direction. Why was she here?

The splash and crest of waves hit the hull, and Lenora dried her tears. The ship steadied along the ocean as they pulled further out to sea. She swallowed, steadier now, but still a little ill.

Pushing to her trembling legs, Lenora scanned the ship. She wanted to find where the men had stored her pet axolotl to ensure it hadn't toppled over in the bumpy launch. In front of Lenora, the open deck teemed with sailors busy with various tasks. Behind her was the wheel of the ship, and beyond that a single, small cabin lined with windows in the same fine wood as the rest of the ship.

Where were the stairs below deck? She scanned the area again, deciding they must be near the cabin and out of her line of vision. Not thinking of her surroundings and the steady flow of men along the deck of the ship, she turned quickly on her heel.

She collided with a man's chest, bouncing backwards and smacking her rear end on the floor.

"Oww," she groaned.

Above her, Captain Devonshire stood with his arms crossed, frowning. Unlike yesterday, he wore a navy three-sided hat and a light-colored muslin blouse with loose-fitting tan breeches.

Relief flooded Lenora. She was on the right ship.

"You need to watch where you're going."

She searched for some kindness in his dark eyes but saw only gruffness. "I…" Her mind went blank, and her face heated at his criticism.

"Also, why are you wearing that ridiculous gown?" He laughed. "Didn't you think to bring a hat? You'll bake to the color of a lobster in no time. You're already looking pink." He smiled, but she found nothing amusing about their exchange.

This is how he greets his betrothed?

She had hoped his appeal to the minister on her behalf was a sign of his kindness.

Apparently not.

She opened her mouth to respond, taken aback by his sheer rudeness, when he dropped his hat on her head and pulled her to her feet in one swift motion.

"Has anyone shown you your quarters?"

She swallowed. "No."

He walked off, and she followed, unable to do anything else. As she expected, the stairs going below deck were right in front of the cabin. They were difficult to see until she was close. There was no railing, just an opening in the deck with narrow stairs, leading under the sailing vessel.

Her heart thrummed. She wanted to confront the captain about the arrangement he had made with her father – why he wanted her here before their marriage. Her face flushed hot, thinking of unsavory implications, and she twisted the skirt of her silken gown between her fingers.

The underbelly of the ship was dark. After being out in the bright light of day, Lenora could barely see a thing, but there was some sort of unnatural luminescence that she assumed had been procured from magical means from another country.

Several boards along the ceiling beamed with soft light, not unlike moonlight. She gasped. Living in Oceanea amongst other humans, she hadn't experienced anything of the sort before, but pirates had the opportunity to travel all of Lurin. Running her hand along the smooth planks, she tried to detect where the light came from, but the glowing wood appeared as normal as the rest of the ship, not even warm to the touch.

The captain opened the first doorway on his left, and he stepped inside the small room, gesturing for her to follow. It was hardly bigger than her kitchen's pantry, completely wooden and windowless, with a single bed frame, desk, and chair. Her trunk had been shoved into the corner. The only light came from the radiance of the wood, which she prayed didn't continue all night long.

Devonshire looked at her, and she flushed, becoming acutely aware of being alone with her new fiancé.

He frowned, pointing at the bed's headboard – if the stark metal could be counted as such. Her axolotl's tank had two belts strapped around it and looped to a metal crossbeam of the lower part of the bed frame.

"He seemed important." Devonshire gestured at Loxi. "Sometimes cast off can be rough, especially if we encounter any sirens. Sorry, I didn't greet you... After yesterday's reaction, I wasn't expecting you to come, but I'm glad you have." He rubbed the back of his neck. "When I saw the tank and your belongings, I hurried down here to secure him."

She warmed at his words and wanted to thank him for his efforts on Loxi's behalf, but instead her curiosity won over. "Sirens?" She knew of the sea monsters and overheard rumors of magical creatures in other realms of Lurin, but she'd never heard the word "siren."

He quirked an eyebrow. "What do you call the demons?"

"Are you referring to the sea monsters?" she asked in a hushed tone.

"Why are you whispering?"

Her face heated again, going from pink to red. "Ladies aren't permitted to speak on politics."

"That's ludicrous." He scratched at his tan, whiskered chin, leaning lazily against the wall. She was surprised he was the captain. He couldn't be more than a few years older than herself.

She gawked. "Some sliver of decorum is necessary, don't you think?"

He frowned, stiffening. "As the wife of a sea captain, I don't think you need to bother with such things anymore."

Her heart beat faster. "Fiancée," she corrected. "And what should I bother with?"

His smile returned. "I have work to do. Enjoy your new quarters. You may go anywhere on the ship, except for my cabin." He pulled the door shut behind himself as he left, and Lenora realized he hadn't answered her question.

Lenora spun in a circle. The room was utilitarian, hardly befitting of a woman of her station, even with the faint magical glow. She slumped down on her cot before jolting to her feet. A sharp pain pierced her backside. The offending spring snagged the back of her dress, tearing a hole in the silken fabric.

Lenora fingered it and sobbed. What was she doing on this horrible ship? She'd had a chance to escape – they'd nearly left without her, yet in the end she'd come willingly.

She sank to the floor. Like the rest of the ship, the room was encased in fine dark wood. While she'd admired it from the shore, in this windowless room, it felt depressing. Among the minimal furniture, there was no wardrobe nor a mirror. She supposed her belongings would have to stay stuffed in her overly full trunk.

She pressed a finger on the side of Loxi's tank. The axolotl swam over to it for a moment, making her smile.

Her fiancé – no, the *pirate* – had ensured her pet axolotl's safety, which showed he was capable of kindness. She let out a shaky breath, wiping away a few rogue tears. Feeling sorry for herself would get her nowhere. She stripped off her damaged dress with great effort, knocking the captain's hat to the ground. Scoping it up once more, she stroked the hat's soft material. It was a great deal finer than she would've expected for a pirate, and he had been thoughtful to give it to her, even if he hadn't been polite about it.

Digging in her trunk, she removed nearly half her dresses before finding a more suitable cotton frock she could slip on herself. Without a lady's maid, she'd be unable to wear most of her gowns that required a second set of hands. She sighed, smoothing the loose, blown-tresses of her up-do – another vanity she'd be unable to replicate on her own – and went above deck.

Chapter Six
The Crew

Lenora stared over the vast blue ocean and smiled. She had felt abandoned by the Maker after her heartbreak over Thomas, but her beautiful surroundings reminded her that the Maker was with her in this strange new place and this strange new life, even if she felt distant from Him.

She had always loved the ocean, and although this wasn't the life she would've chosen for herself, she hummed with renewed purpose.

A life at sea was a life of adventure.

Scanning the deck for her intended, Lenora walked along the edges of the ship. She'd already adjusted to the gentle bump and sway of the water.

It was odd being engaged to a complete stranger, maybe even more peculiar that she had no idea what he expected of her. He said decorum didn't matter, then what did?

The fact that he'd brought her to her own quarters suggested that he didn't expect to become familiar with her too quickly.

Good.

She blushed, pushing the thought from her mind as she paced, intending to learn the layout of her new home. Lenora took in the shimmering view of the ocean while studying the pirates. The crew relaxed, chatting with one another or playing card games.

But no one glanced in her direction.

She made a loop of the enormous deck, and no one offered her as much as a "hello." A wave of homesickness stole over her. Even though she had lived an isolated life at her father's manor, she'd had visitors, the season's parties, and her father's loyal staff.

Father.

When would she see him again? His betrayal still stung, but most of her previous anger was overtaken by her loneliness.

She had no idea where they were sailing nor when they planned to return. Tears burned behind her eyes, but she forced them down. She couldn't bear the idea of appearing weak.

Out of the corner of her eye, a young man with a mop sidled up to her. Turning in greeting, Lenora planted a smile on her face. "Oh, hello there. I'm Lenora, what's your –"

He looked not a day over thirteen, skinny but tall with unevenly cut sandy blonde hair and deeply tanned skin, like the rest of the crew. Before answering, he thrust the mop and bucket into her hands.

"I'm Leopold, 'Mam. If you're to be one of us, then you best get to work."

"Surely, the captain wouldn't want his betrothed –"

"Captain's orders."

She gasped, dropping the bucket and its soapy contents everywhere.

Leopold winked. "I'll get ya more. Best not waste it again, though, or you'll get on the captain's bad side."

Squeezing the handle of the mop, Lenora let out a huff, pushing the wet puddle away from her feet and hemline. The edge was already soaked, and she considered changing again when Leopold was back with another bucket.

He frowned. "Haven't you ever used a mop before?"

"No, of course not!" she shrieked.

He chuckled, taking the mop back and demonstrating. "You don't have to grip her so tight, just sweep her around, like this."

She smirked. "The mop's a female?"

"Exactly. Way too many men on this ship. Glad to have you with us. I miss my sisters." He sighed.

"Do you get to see them often?"

"Never."

Her heart constricted, thinking of Father and Hettie. "I'm so sorry."

He shrugged. "Life of a sailor." He went back to mopping. She relaxed, thinking she was off the hook when he hadn't handed it back to her. "I think I've demonstrated enough. I'm in charge of swabbing that end." He pointed at the front of the ship. "You do here to the stern."

"Stern?"

"The back."

He started to walk away.

"Wait!" she cried.

Leopold turned his head.

"Can you tell me where we're going?"

He smiled, revealing several missing teeth. "Only the captain knows the answer to that."

Leopold had made the task look easy, but her hands and wrists ached with the effort of pushing the mop along the wooden surface. She frowned. The deck hardly looked dirty. Would anyone notice if she quit? She tapped her nails along the handle. Dropping the mop, she intended to give Devonshire a piece of her mind.

Captain's orders? She was a lady!

She reached his cabin, ready to knock, when the ship jostled. The crew scrambled to their posts. The sky was clear blue, and the wind was steady. Uninterrupted ocean stretched in every direction.

Her heart squeezed in her chest.

There was nothing to explain the sudden change except the sea monsters. Should she escape beneath the deck?

Her pulse thrummed, and she twitched with nerves.

But she was also highly curious.

The pirates had some way to avoid the creatures' detection to survive out here. Surely, her father hadn't allowed her to be thrust into this kind of danger without being assured of her safety?

The ship rolled to one side, knocking her from her feet. She screamed, expecting to be thrown into the ocean.

Captain Devonshire strode by her without so much as a glance, barking orders and clapping his hands together.

Was he excited for the attack? The men grabbed onto ropes and harpoons, stowed beneath the edges of the ship, but Lenora noticed most were smiling, laughing. Her stomach churned with every slap of the waves. Sea water splashed her face. "This can't be normal!" she screamed to no one in particular.

Scrambling along the deck and soaked in salt water, Lenora clung to the nearest mast, hanging on for dear life as the ship pitched and bumped.

Whoops of the rowdy pirates grated on her nerves. Her arms trembled with exertion.

A murmur of moans greeted the leveling of the ship.

Lenora exhaled a breath and pushed herself back to standing on her wobbly legs.

Captain Devonshire addressed the crew, "We'll get 'em next time, boys!"

She thought he might pause and explain, but he walked by her once more, slamming his cabin door behind himself. She followed.

"Captain," Lenora called out, knocking at his door.

He ignored her.

She tried the handle, but it was locked. She walked around the perimeter of the cabin, peeking in on him through the evenly spaced glass windows. He sat at his desk with his head in his hands. After trying the door again, she tapped at a pane with her nail and yelled, "Captain, can I speak with you, please?"

He unlocked his door, returning to his desk. "Come in," he answered gruffly. His long brown hair was pulled back neatly, contrasting with his rough, unkempt crewmates. His bronzed skin and dark features contrasted with his light-colored clothing. She hovered inside the doorway, studying him. Although she'd been pushy, she felt awkward now that she had his full attention.

His deep brown eyes sparkled with curiosity. He lifted a single eyebrow. "Well, what is it?"

Lenora twisted at the drenched skirt of her dress. "Was that one of the sea monsters?"

"Aye."

"Um, why were you all so… gleeful?"

He smiled, dimpling a cheek. "That's your urgent question?" He laughed. "We hunt them. Oceanea gives us a hefty price for each head."

Lenora drew her hands to her own neck. "H-head?"

"Of the demons. To help keep Oceanea safe." His smile faltered. "There's less of us out here than there used to be, and the sirens keep increasing. As you saw, even when we find them. It's not a sure thing…"

"You go looking for them." Her eyes widened.

"Yes."

The clock behind his mahogany desk ticked. It was made entirely of shells, reminding her of her family's ballroom chandelier.

"Wait, so you don't steal riches from passing ships?"

"Oh, I suppose you think we have buried treasure too?" His brown eyes twinkled mischievously.

Was he making a joke?

"I don't understand… Why do they call you pirates?"

"Most of us were pirates at one time or another. Your father recruited me. I enjoy hunting more than stealing, and I'm glad for the honest work. Besides, no one sails this far south anymore, so we have nothing to steal." He must've read the concern on her face because he added, "Even if there were, I can assure you our pirating days are behind us, and my crew kills nothing but fish for dinner and the demons to protect our country."

"I didn't think pirates swore fealty to anything."

"They don't, but most of them have families or friends in Oceanea they'd like to keep safe, and once a pirate always a pirate… at least in terms of work. There aren't jobs on land for men who've spent their lives at sea."

She sat on the open chair on the other side of the desk, attempting to pull it closer, but like everything else on the ship, it was bolted down. "Why don't more people know this?"

He shrugged. "Your father doesn't want the citizens to be afraid, and like I said, most of us are former pirates or rebels who couldn't find work after the war. The title doesn't offend us."

Without thinking, she blurted, "What do the sirens look like?" Her face flushed at her own impudence, but after years of being unable to ask such questions, it was refreshing.

His eyes widened a moment. "I think it's best if you stay below deck during an attack. They're horrible creatures."

She licked her lips, emboldened by his willingness to answer her questions. "Captain, why am I here?"

She thought he would answer, but instead, he checked his pocket watch and left.

"Wait!"

Pausing at the doorway, Devonshire frowned at her. "I need to be going. Percy is steering, and the old man is known to drag us off course."

"I'm not really expected to mop, am I?" She forced a laugh.

"Aye, my lady." He winked, ushering her to the door before shutting himself back inside the cabin.

Chapter Seven
The Monsters

"Demons fifty clicks port!" Percy shouted from the crow's nest before scrambling down to join the rest of the crew.

He was one of the few sailors who had bothered sharing his name with her, though she couldn't exactly call the old man friendly.

Days at sea had given Lenora no more answers than when she had first arrived, so despite her fear, she made her way to the side of the ship, peering into the splashes of waves.

Leopold handed her a harpoon with a nod. Lenora knew that the captain wouldn't approve, but she was determined to learn more about her new way of life.

This was Lenora's fifth day at sea, so far she had learned three things:

1. The sailors lived for hunting the sea monsters.
2. They barely spoke of anything else.
3. Her fiancé barely spoke to anyone.

Lenora hadn't heard one word from Devonshire since her first day aboard when she forced herself into his cabin.

Since then, he had managed to elude her, and she considered whether he was hiding from her.

Sometimes she'd catch the captain looking at her, but if she tried to approach him, he'd hurry away, making her feel like she'd imagined the whole thing.

She didn't know what he wanted a wife for, as he seemed uninterested in any sort of companionship. Part of her thought she should be relieved. She wasn't sure how to be the wife of a former pirate and siren hunter, but she was lonely.

Her entire adolescence drilled into her the importance of getting married, providing heirs, and establishing a welcoming home. Without a home or an attentive husband, she wasn't sure how to do either. Would the captain change after they officially married? Women of Oceanea gossiped about such things – everyone knew it was foolhardy to expect a man to modify his ways.

Her new life was so vastly different from what she'd been trained to do. There were no opportunities to dress up, nor tea times to prepare, nor the entertaining of guests. Hettie had packed Lenora's needlework, but she didn't see the point. Instead, she filled her days mopping and staring out at the ocean.

She'd balked at the chore at first, but she didn't have anything to do with her time anyway.

Leopold was the only one who even tried speaking to her. Most of the others only grunted when she asked them questions.

A wave soaked her face, washing into her mouth and causing her to choke. She gripped the harpoon tighter as she thought of facing a sea monster.

The water swirled, pulling the ship into a spin. Her pulse roared in her ears. She thought they'd raise the sails again to pull out of it, but every sailor stood with a harpoon in hand along the sides of the ship.

Black shadows flickered in and out of her vision. Was this the sea monster, or siren, as Devonshire called them?

A clawed hand jetted from the water, and Lenora tumbled backwards, biting back a scream. She clambered to her feet.

The hand was nearly an eighth of the size of the ship, almost as large as the tail of a whale. She'd pictured the creatures with scales and fins or tentacles, but the hand looked almost human.

Her stomach tightened as the shadows became more defined. The dark lines were strands of hair snaking through the surface of the water.

The siren's head grew larger and larger before her. How big was this creature?

Percy cheered, rushing toward it, clearly enjoying himself.

Lenora's eyes widened.

"Cover your ears!" Leopold shrieked.

"Wh-what?" Before she had time to ask more, the siren emerged.

For a moment, she thought she observed dark sunken eyes and a circular mouth with jagged teeth, but then the sea monster shifted to the form of a woman with alabaster skin, raven hair, and ocean blue eyes. She was nearly the size of a whale, and Lenora dreaded what she could do to their ship. The siren curled her red lips, smiling and singing.

"Weary sailors
Let us bring you rest
Stop your toiling
Believe what is best

Relax, visit
In the ocean deep
Never striving
Lying down to sleep."

Lenora gasped as she watched several men drop their weapons and dive into the ocean after her. Leopold kept his ears covered with his hands, watching the chaos unfold. Lenora gripped her weapon tighter.

The towering woman emerging from the sea was beautiful. Her warm smile and kind eyes were inviting. The song soothed her, like a long, forgotten lullaby of her mother's. But then the image flickered, and she could see the horrible, monstrous creature again.

Leopold's hands were still clapped to the sides of his head as he kicked at her harpoon. "Throw it, Lenora!"

The ship lurched, followed by an ear-splitting shriek. Rough arms yanked her backwards, just as she had managed to take aim. The captain dragged her across the deck, slamming and locking his cabin door.

"I almost had it!" she huffed.

He didn't answer her.

She scowled until she was knocked off her feet as the ship swayed. Devonshire closed the distance, catching her.

"Th-thank you."

He smiled, and her cheeks burned under his attention.

He removed his hat and gestured to his ears. A bandage was wrapped around his head, holding gobs of cotton in place.

"I CAN'T HEAR YOU," he shouted, releasing her. "I APOLOGIZE FOR NOT MAKING SURE THE CREW SECURED YOUR EARS. THE DEMONS LURE SAILORS TO THEIR DEATHS. AS YOU SAW, SOME OF THE CREW FORGOT THEIR OWN BANDAGES."

She thought of her momentary vision of the beautiful woman. Although the feeling had passed, there was a moment when the sea monster had felt inviting. Was this the creature's power? She'd seen at least a handful of sailors jump overboard.

He continued, "I'M GLAD YOU'RE ALRIGHT."

She snorted.

He smiled, tipping his head and taking in her reaction.

Despite not looking like any other gentleman she'd ever known, she had to admit he was rather handsome in his own way. His tall height, tanned skin, dark hair and eyes, and square jaw contrasted with the less intimidating, soft, pale geniality of her previous suitors. Before she had time to process that last thought, however, the captain backed out of the room, locking her inside.

"Hey!" she shouted, kicking at the door and yanking at the knob. "Let me out!"

She slumped against the door.

Her dress was tattered and filthy. She studied her hands and gasped. Her nails were even worse, and her palms were turning rough. If her father could see her now! Did she even resemble a lady anymore, or after nearly a week at sea, did she look more like a pirate?

The ship swayed as the sounds of fighting met her ears. She was surprised by her jealousy. She was much safer inside the captain's cabin, but she felt like she was missing out on an important adventure.

Pressing her ear to the door, she heard the siren's song. She knocked harder against the door until her knuckles hurt.

The ship shook, and she was thrown from her feet. Shouts of men and stomping along the deck blended with screaming, more singing, and splashes. Her heart squeezed in her chest as she held onto the captain's chair. Her body shifted along the ground of the cabin as the boat was tossed to and fro.

How was the crew faring? The captain? If something happened to him, would she be returned home?

She chewed her lip. Even with their distant relationship, she didn't want that. Thinking of his rough grip pulling her into the cabin stirred something inside her. He did care for her safety.

Was it possible he held affections for her?

She'd caught his distant gaze more than once; the softness in his expression was akin to the desire she'd caught from other suitors. But why didn't he call on her? Why keep his distance?

The ship bumped, throwing her into the air along with the few items scattered across the captain's desk. Lenora screamed. The noises of battle swelled, cutting through the thick cabin walls, and she was tempted to bang against the door again.

The ship settled, and she loosened her grip, cautiously standing on her wobbly legs. Lenora's pulse slowed, and she pressed her ear to the door again. Celebratory shouts replaced the previous distressed screams until the noise outside quieted.

No one came for her. She paced the room. Had she been forgotten?

So much time passed that she searched around the cabin for something to occupy her thoughts, returning the parchment and quills to the desk that had been dispersed about the room.

She thrummed her fingers along its smooth surface before searching inside.

The captain's desk was locked, but after jiggling the drawer a few times, it jetted forth with a satisfying thump. Inside was a pipe, a tin of tobacco, a jar of ink, another quill, and a small leather journal.

She flipped it open, expecting a log of travels.

Another day at sea. We've only taken down one demon in months. What more is there to say? I long for someone to share my thoughts with, other than this crew of men, but the job we're doing for the country of Oceanea outweighs my personal desires.

She paused, her face heating. This entry was dated a year ago. Captain Devonshire had dreamed of a companion, much in the same way she had. Did he truly want her here? Why did he stay away from her and not share some of these thoughts he alluded to? She hardly saw him interact with anyone, other than to bark out orders.

She held the journal to her chest.

Maybe there was more to her betrothed than she had gleaned.

A click at the door sounded, and she hastily shoved the journal in the drawer, slamming it shut, trying to wipe away any sign of what she'd read from her face.

As the door flung open, her heart sank.

Leopold instructed, "Better come out, Miss Lenora. There's a heap of clean-up to do."

Chapter Eight
The Clean-up

Lenora gagged.

Blood and gore mixed with seawater sloshed over the surface of the deck. The noises of battle hadn't prepared her for the gruesome aftermath.

"What happened after the captain dragged me away?"

Leopold whistled. "We killed the beast."

Percy whooped, clapping Leopold on the back as he walked by the pair of them on his way back up to the crow's nest.

Lenora nodded. She knew it was an admirable feat, yet something like sympathy burned in her gut. She'd seen and heard firsthand how the sirens aimed to lure them to drowning, but the idea of anything spilling this much blood made her flinch.

"How did you kill it?" She forced herself to ask.

"A steady stream of harpoons."

"And are you sure it is?"

Leopold raised his brows.

"Dead," she clarified. "I can see the blood, but I don't see the head." She swallowed. "The captain mentioned he keeps them… as proof."

"The creatures shrink to the size of humans when they die, and aye, we have the body on board. We only take the head when we can't grab the whole thing or run out of space."

Lenora shivered.

Leopold frowned, not unkindly. "My sisters would've scolded me for talking to a fine lady about such things."

"Well, I asked you to."

Leopold gestured to the deck. "We have a giant mess on our hands today."

She groaned. Her arms were pink with sun, her palms blistered, and she was exhausted. "I was hoping for some bunk time after all the excitement."

"Okay, don't stay away too long though." He sighed. "I don't relish the idea of mopping up this mess by myself."

She exited quickly before Leopold could change his mind, grabbing a bucket of water from the wash barrel and excusing herself below deck. She wasn't sure she could clean the deck and not get sick.

Loxi bumped against the edge of his tank in greeting.

"Miss me, boy?"

She pulled off her tattered and stained gown. At this pace, she'd run out of clothes in no time. She hadn't cleaned herself since coming aboard, and she hated the thought that she probably stunk as much as some of the men. Finding a set of towels tucked away in her trunk, she washed herself head to toe. Thinking of the bloody mess above ship, she shuddered, scrubbing herself harder. She forced herself to stop, sore from her fervent scouring, and selected a long-sleeved gown. It would be warm but help protect her pink arms.

She washed her hair last, making a mess of her floor, and wringing it out back into the bucket. She brushed at her tangled curls before sweeping them into a low bun to make way for Devonshire's hat.

He hadn't asked for it back, and she took this as another sign of his hidden kindness.

She curled up on her side, intending to rest, but thoughts of the day's attack kept her stirring.

Leopold had said the body of the siren was on board. She wondered if it resembled the monster she'd first seen or the alluring woman.

Loxi thumped against his tank several times more, and she realized she'd forgotten to feed him today. A barrel of small feeder fish was kept further down the hall.

She stretched, lacing her heeled boots before walking down the long underbelly of the ship.

There were only four doors other than her own: two led to the large, open crew quarters crammed with rows upon rows of bunks, and one held a large pantry of all the ship's food and provisions. The fourth, at the very end of the hall, she hadn't been shown. Biting at the inside of her cheek, she stared at the unmarked door.

She backtracked to the crews' quarters. Glancing inside, she confirmed they were empty before tiptoeing to the last door.

No one came in or out of this room. She hadn't even thought to check it before this moment, but her curiosity won. Where else would they stash the bodies of sirens? Her hand quaked as she tried the knob. It was locked.

Of course it was.

She jiggled it again, thinking of the captain's desk, shoving her shoulder into the corner, but it didn't budge. She tried a second time before grabbing Loxi's lunch from the pantry and heading back to her room.

What was wrong with her? Why did she want to see the body anyway? She trembled, trying to push away her morbid thoughts.

Loxi gobbled his meal down, and she rubbed at her brow. Had she remembered to feed him the day before? She needed to take better care of him. The unchanging view and monotonous chores made the days blur together. The tank's top was still slid open.

Loxi sprang from the water, and Lenora yelped. Though axolotls could undergo metamorphosis, it was dangerous for them to leave the water. Many of the delicate creatures didn't survive the process. She extended her palm, intending to drop him back into his tank when he winked.

She blinked. Was her loneliness getting the better of her? She brought the salamander to eye level, and his affixed smile widened, opening into a full toothless grin.

"Loxi?" she asked. "Can you understand me?" Her heart beat faster. The salamander slithered off her hand, diving into his open tank.

Her pulse slowed, and she chuckled at herself, sliding the lid in place. She sighed, hesitating a moment more. It wasn't right for her to keep hiding away. She hoped Leopold would be done, but thinking of the extraordinary mess, she doubted it. Shaking out her arms and legs, she forced herself to put one foot in front of the other and return to the deck.

***

The sun began to set on the horizon, shining rays of red and gold across the glistening water. This was the best part of being at sea.

More time had passed than she realized while she was below deck. The polished ship gleamed in the sun, and Leopold sat around with a group of men, playing a game of cards.

"Sorry for not helping earlier. I must've fallen asleep. I-I really didn't want to help, but I had no idea how much time passed. Thank you, Leopold. It must've been horrible."

He shrugged. "It wasn't fun, but thank the captain. He told me to let you rest."

She scanned the deck. "That was kind of him," she said almost to herself. "Where is he?"

"Probably locked away in the cabin," sighed the man to Leopold's right.

"I'd like to thank him for his generosity."

"Good luck with that," shot Percy. "He always steals himself away after the attacks."

She nodded, sitting next to Leopold. "Why is that?"

Leopold whistled. "None of us know."

She removed her hat and unraveled her damp hair with her fingers. "What can you all tell me about him?"

A gray-haired man spoke, "He's a mighty fine Captain, feeds us and pays us better than any I've had, and lets us go ashore."

Murmurs of agreement rose from the gathered men.

Percy nodded. "Aye, he took me in after a siren killed my former crew."

"Oh, Percy, that's –"

"And he doesn't keep Oceanea's gold for himself," another sailor, who appeared to be missing all his teeth, interrupted.

Percy continued, "Uses it all for supplies, repairs, and his crew. Not a finer man anywhere."

"Who?" The deep, bellow of Captain Devonshire startled Lenora. She turned, wanting to read his expression, but the setting sun cast his figure in shadow.

Leopold smiled. "We're telling your future bride a bit about the man she's going to marry."

"Well, don't."

He turned and left, stomping back to his cabin. Lenora's stomach plummeted. The group of them watched until the door slammed, and the sailors turned back to their card game.

Chapter Nine
Another Attack

Lenora dreamed she was rolling down a grassy hill outside her family's manor. Gasping awake, she smacked against the far wall. The dramatic sway of the ship meant they were either caught in a storm or another siren attack.

Based on her exhaustion, Lenora guessed only a few hours had passed since she'd gone to bed. She hadn't been expecting another siren today, and she wondered if it came seeking them out in retribution. As a precaution, she folded clean stockings around her ears and then secured them tightly with a ribbon before emerging from her room.

The hallway was packed as the men filed above board on the single, narrow staircase that led to the deck. Lenora squeezed in line, not wanting to miss another chance to see the monsters. So much of her life, she'd been tucked away in the security of her father's manor, but she longed for adventure. She knew it was unladylike to seek out danger, but her entire life had been influenced by these creatures, and she needed to face them. A faint shriek hummed through her stockings, making her consider returning to the safety of her room.

In the night sky, the light of the moon and stars illuminated the monster hanging along the tipping bow of the ship. One clawed hand grabbed at a mast while its head pressed flat on the deck.

The sound of splintering wood carried through the air, and Lenora held her breath.

Looming feathery wings flapped, followed by the splashing of a massive fish-like tail behind it. The wings were blood-red and terrifying to look at – a warning of the death to come if you crossed the creature. The siren was attempting to climb onboard or sink the whole ship – Lenora couldn't tell which. It's dark hair snaked along the newly polished surface grabbing at men and tossing them into the sea.

Lenora gasped, freezing in front of the stairs before she was shoved out of the way.

Her hands trembled and her wobbly legs disobeyed her fearful mind as she tried to join her fellow crewmen along the sides of the ship.

She took a deep breath in and out.

She needed to secure a weapon and stay away from the creature's grasp. This was her home too, and if this demon sank the ship, she'd drown with the rest of them. Her mother's funeral flashed into her mind, and she shook it away.

Lenora ran starboard, patting down the side of the ship where the weapons were secured, but all the harpoons were already taken. The ship tipped forward as the siren threw another hand on the mast. The railing of the ship snapped, breaking under the weight of the creature. Giant splashes washed along the deck as she beat her tail against the ocean. The ship was nearly at a forty-five degree angle now. Barrels and crates crashed into the water. Men not holding on, slid across the slick surface.

Lenora was glad that she hadn't taken the time to lace up her heeled boots with their smooth bottoms – her sweaty, bare feet helped her scale the wooden planks. Scrambling along the sides, she kept searching for a weapon. She exhaled as her hand fell on a lone harpoon, possibly the last, and raised it in the direction of the monster nearly fifty yards away from her.

She prayed to the Maker for the men thrown into the deep, for their safety or a quick death, and for bravery.

But she couldn't make herself rush at the creature.

She swallowed the bile rising in her throat and allowed gravity to slide her forward. Aiming for the center of the creature's head, she drew back her harpoon and threw it with all her might.

It landed several yards short.

What had Lenora expected? If she survived this night, she vowed to practice with the weapon daily.

The creature jerked its head to the side, shaking the entire ship with a tremble as it shivered back to its smaller size. Lenora remembered what Leopold had said, the creatures shrank when they died, and she let out the breath she'd been holding. The ship bobbed, nearly launching Lenora into the air, with the sudden shift in the loss of weight.

Pulling the stockings from her ears, Lenora ran forward to investigate the slain sea monster.

The captain stood at its side with a bloody harpoon, taking deep gasping breaths.

A cheer rose up from the men, and several clapped Devonshire on the back, as they walked past him.

The siren was the size of a diminutive young girl, and despite Lenora's previous terror, an unwelcome wave of sympathy stole over her. A tarp was dragged over the body before Lenora could look closer, but she'd seen the dead creature had lost its tail and wings.

Devonshire's face was a stony mask. He blinked at Lenora. "Why aren't you in bed?"

"I woke up."

The crew busied themselves around the ship, starting on repairs to the wooden railing.

He tsked. "Why don't you go grab a mop? This whole deck is a mess again. We can't be sliding all over it, though I'm afraid you'll have to do it alone." He grimaced.

She bit back a groan. "Well, it's only fair since Leopold did the whole thing earlier."

He shook his head, not meeting her eyes. "No, Lenora. I say that because Leopold was one of the unfortunate ones."

Leopold?

Her heart felt like it was caving in on itself. *Maker, how could you take Leopold?* He was young, and her only companion close to a friend. She'd known him only a short while, but she couldn't imagine life without him aboard this ship. Tears sprang from her eyes, and she cried out, "No! He can't be… It's not fair."

"Nothing about those demons is fair." His tone was gentle, and his eyes were glassy as they met hers.

He cupped her face as if wanting to say more before hugging her tightly. The affection was so unexpected that her pent up emotion spilled over.

She sobbed against his chest, feeling the thundering of his heartbeat. "I can't believe it."

He rubbed her back. "I'm so sorry, Lenora. It was selfish of me to have you here." His deep voice was choked with emotion, making her sob harder.

But he pulled away, hurrying back in the direction of his cabin and leaving her alone in her grief. Her body was cold in his absence. Did she want the captain's affections?

"Wait!" She commanded, ignoring the stares of the nearby crew. He paused his retreat. "What do you mean it was selfish? Why am I here, Captain?"

He met her eyes. "Do you want to leave?"

She didn't answer.

He waited, his brow furrowed, but she didn't know what to say. His shoulders fell as he retreated to his cabin, and she wished she had an answer for him. His question rang in her ears long after he'd gone. Was he upset she hadn't said no? How could he expect her to say yes?

Lenora threw her hands in the air and grabbed a mop, scouring the deck with intensity.

Her heart swelled, thinking of Devonshire's embrace, and then it broke again, remembering Leopold.

***

She finished mopping by daybreak. Lenora had not noticed the ship turn, but the sun rose along the right side, to the east, showing they were headed north again. More tears burned behind her eyes and down her throat, but she swallowed them, intending to find answers.

Percy climbed from the crow's nest, and she called out to him. "Hey, I have a few questions, and I was hoping you might have some answers for me."

He was already walking away before she'd asked a single one.

"Percy!"

"I'm tired, 'Mam. Headed to my bunk. I suggest you do the same."

"We've changed direction."

He sighed, crossing his arms. "That wasn't a question."

"Okay, fine. Why did we change direction?"

He looked away from her. "To bring the bodies to shore. Some have families who will want them."

"The sirens?"

He dropped his arms, and his singular, furry brow lifted. "No, of course not."

She fidgeted with the skirt of her dress. "No, I mean, what do we do with them?"

"Lord Darlington inspects them himself and pays up."

Father?

Her heart fluttered. She would get to see Father. "He comes on the ship?"

Percy groaned. "No, Captain brings them to shore. Lenora, please, I've been up for more than a day. I'm too tired for more pesky questions."

"Yes, of course, thank you."

The pirate grumbled as he pushed past her and disappeared below the ship. She stared over the water, wanting to catch a glimpse of home, but of course, they were still too far off.

Then she remembered Leopold, no doubt crammed inside the room down the hall from her alongside the sea monsters, and her throat burned. He'd been the only person close to a friend, and now he was gone. She tried to picture his sisters, learning the news of his death. Would they be proud of his sacrifice or angry that he had left them?

Lenora wasn't sure how to feel.

She'd seen firsthand how dangerous the sirens were. Captain Devonshire and his crew provided an invaluable service to their countrymen. Without the pirates, there was no hope of Oceanea ever returning to the ocean, and the coastal country greatly depended on its fishing and trade for survival.

But Leopold…

His death was wrong.

She wiped at the tears tracing their way down her chin as she stared across the glowing sunrise on the water, praying and clinging to the promise of a new day.

Chapter Ten
Loneliness

No one spoke of Leopold.

Somehow, that made the loss worse. She'd only known him a short while, yet she seemed to be the only one grieving. As she mopped, several crew members marched by with their heads down, ignoring her presence. Lenora gave up trying to start a conversation with them – they always responded in grunts.

A hollow ache began in her chest that pulsated throughout her entire body.

She sometimes imagined him, mopping at the other end of the ship. His brief presence in her life had left a strong imprint, like a brand upon her heart. Leopold.

Was this her life?

Quiet, empty days, staring out at the same endless blue water?

She missed Leopold. She missed home, Hettie, and Father. And Thomas.

One moment, she hated him with a boiling intensity, and the next, she longed for his company. She knew she shouldn't, but her own betrothed felt like a stranger. Their interactions would hardly be considered courting, let alone husband and wife.

She thought of the warmth of Devonshire's arms.

There were moments he showed his affections and kindness, but then he snatched them away so quickly, she'd wonder if she dreamed them.

She wanted someone to talk to and confide in. She prayed to the Maker, wondering if He ever bothered to hear her prayers. Wondering if her creator cared enough to listen.

Leaning on her mop, she hovered nearby while a group played cards. She felt someone's eyes on her. Devonshire stood several feet away, but as soon as she met his gaze, he hurried off. She sighed. Maybe she'd just imagined it. Had she hurt him when she hadn't answered his question? It had been days since Leopold's death, and he'd kept his distance since that night.

"I win." Percy grinned, laying out his cards on top of the barrel.

The man to his left grunted, taking up the cards again and reshuffling them. The other men in the circle passed Percy gold; a few quit, muttering.

"Can I play?" Lenora asked.

Percy nodded, and the rest of the others stood up and left. She blinked back tears, surprised by the effect their coldness still had on her.

"Why do they hate me?"

Percy grunted, dealing her cards. "How much gold do you have?"

She shook her head. "None."

"Ehh! Ya can't play cards then. What's the point?" Percy stood, stretching his back.

She watched him go, her limbs weighing heavy at her sides.

Grabbing her evening bucket of fresh water, she went below deck. The other sailors didn't wash, but no one had told her she shouldn't. Devonshire appeared cleaner and smelled better than the rest of them, so she suspected he did the same.

She would need to figure out a way to launder her dresses soon. The dirty gowns were taking over her cramped room.

Loxi splashed in his tank, and she sank beside him on the floor. "Do you like it here, Loxi?"

The axolotl thunked against the top of the tank.

"I can't let you out again. It's not safe."

She sighed, drawing up her knees.

He tapped again, and her resolve waned. She decided to open the lid.

Loxi crawled out, staring at her.

"Are you happy I opened your tank?"

The axolotl nodded, and Lenora gasped. "Can you understand me?"

The salamander nodded again.

Lenora chewed her lip. She'd always felt a close connection to her pet, but now she considered whether the days of loneliness had driven her mad. She swallowed. "Do you like your tank?"

Loxi shook his head vigorously from side to side.

She laughed, extending her hand for him to climb on. "I'm sorry I haven't spent much time down here with you."

The axolotl blinked its small, round eyes, listening intently.

"I promise I'll come down here more from now on."

He shook his head again.

"No? You don't want me to? Then what do you want?" Lenora didn't expect an answer, but the salamander surprised her again by pointing with his tail.

It jabbed upward.

"You want to go above deck with me?"

Loxi nodded.

"I'd love that, but I'm not sure I should keep you out of the water so long."

In answer, Loxi leapt from her hand and splashed into her bucket.

"Oh!" She laughed. "I guess that'll work."

Lenora slipped on a dress from her dwindling supply of clean clothing, not bothering to close the complicated fasteners along the back before stepping into the hall with bucket in hand.

"I'm not sure where you want me to take you, Loxi," Lenora whispered, feeling like a mad woman, as she stepped up the last of the stairs above board. "It's not as if you can see anything from inside a bucket."

In answer, Loxi scaled up the wooden sides, peeking his small head out. He sniffed at the air, his smile parting.

Lenora looked over the unending blue with him. "It is beautiful, but I've already grown sick of it." The ship was motionless, and the water was flat and waveless. She stared at the sails. They limped on the masts.

She'd already done her work for the day. The deck sparkled, shining in the sun. Without a breeze, the heat was stifling.

"What now, Loxi?"

The salamander swam on his back, gesturing at his stomach with his tail.

"Lunch it is."

Lenora walked below deck to the supply closet, intending to grab a feeder fish for Loxi and whatever she could eat without cooking, but she paused again by the unmarked door.

She asked Loxi, "Why do you think they keep it locked?"

He ignored her, swimming dizzying circles, and she continued on her way inside the pantry. She located a strip of dried meat and some rock-hard bread for herself before prying open the bucket of fish for Loxi.

He gobbled it quickly, asking for more by gesturing to his stomach with his tail. "Uh-uh, just cause you're talking now doesn't mean I'll start over-feeding you." Loxi flicked his tail along the surface, splashing at her defiantly before settling in the bottom of his bucket. She supposed that meant he was angry.

She dropped her food into her pockets before grabbing the bucket. She paused at the unmarked door again before returning to her room.

A knock at her door made her squeak, and she could hear Devonshire's low chuckle in the hallway. "I'm sorry I startled you."

She cracked the door, narrowing her eyes at him. "Why are you here?" She supposed she should be thankful, but she was too cross to extend pleasantries. "You ignore me for days, and then you show up like we're friends."

The smile slid off his sun-kissed face. He sighed, dropping his head.

She bit her tongue, regretting her brazen words, but he surprised her.

"You're right. I shouldn't be avoiding you. I'm sorry."

"Wh-what?" She clutched the door frame, letting the door open fully.

He leaned toward her, causing her to step back into her room. His hands clenched at his sides, and something ticked in his jaw. "I had hoped your father would explain… When I saw your panic at the ceremony, I wanted to call the whole thing off. You don't deserve this. You deserve… I don't know, something better than a life amongst pirates and sirens." He shook his head, turning back in the direction he came.

"No, wait!"

He arched a single brow. "Yes?" His lazy smile returned, and her stomach clenched. Why did his sporadic attentiveness move her so?

"I… I'm not entirely regretful I came aboard."

He laughed. "Is that a compliment?"

She huffed in response, blowing loose strands from her face. Why did he have to be so difficult?

"No," his tone softened, reaching his hands toward hers and squeezing. "I mean, if it is, I'll take it. I'm glad you're here, Lenora."

Chapter Eleven
Stuck

Lenora felt she'd dreamed their previous conversation when Devonshire circumvented her presence the next few days. This morning, he hovered a short distance away, staring at Lenora as she emerged from below deck. Every time she'd tried to speak with him, he slipped away, but this time she was determined to confront him. She sprinted, grabbing his arm as he attempted to retreat to his cabin.

He cleared his throat. His brown eyes sparkled mischievously in the bright sunlight. "Can I help you, Lenora?"

"Why are you avoiding me?"

The captain pulled away, walking by her without an answer. She caught his arm again, trying a different question. "Why isn't the ship moving?" Her face heated as he smiled at her, and she released his arm. She'd never been this forceful with anyone before, but his avoidance after a glimpse of what their relationship could be had transformed her.

"There's no wind. We're stuck until the weather changes."

"For how long?"

"No one knows." He shrugged, frowning.

"What?" Lenora covered her mouth.

The captain went to his cabin, and she followed him, refusing to let him avoid her any longer.

"I demand answers!"

He sat at his desk and squeezed the bridge of his nose. "These things happen, Lenora. None of us are thrilled about it, but no one else is panicking."

Days without wind meant their boat was stuck in the water. She knew she shouldn't complain. The men alternated between cards and fishing, and the captain was right – none of them seemed the least bit bothered. She mopped and hung out with Loxi and was bored out of her mind.

She paced the cabin. "Where do you sleep?"

"Pardon?"

"I've never thought of it before. I assumed it was in here… but you don't have a bed."

"Yes, I usually sleep in my chair."

"That sounds terribly uncomfortable."

He sighed. "It is." He rubbed at his neck as if to demonstrate.

"Then why?"

"I used to have a bed."

"What happened to it?"

He smirked, revealing his dimples. "It was an engagement gift."

Lenora's face heated in understanding. "I didn't realize you'd given up your room for me."

He lifted his hand, waving it side-to-side, as if waving away her concern. "I know you're used to much finer things. Next time we're on shore, I'll get you a better mattress, maybe a bigger tank for your axolotl."

She smiled at him, and he smiled back. The moment felt warm. Intimate even. He reached out and squeezed her hand.

And then he ruined it.

Clearing his throat, he said, "I need to get back to work."

She frowned. What could he possibly be busy with, stuck out in the middle of nowhere? "No." She crossed her arms and sat on the edge of his desk.

"No?" he asked slowly. "I wouldn't think a lady of your stature would refuse her future husband's request."

"I'm a sailor now, not a lady," she retorted, lifting one eyebrow.

He chuckled. "Good point. Well, then maybe you can help me."

He patted along the underside of his desk, searching for something. He pulled out a roll of parchment, flattening it along the surface. Lenora moved, helping hold it flat. The paper held a grid with markings, but the only thing that was labeled was the jagged line at the left edge of the paper.

Lenora recognized it from other maps she'd seen of Lurin and ran her finger along the edge. "Oceanea's coast. So what are the rest of these markings in the ocean?"

A scattering of hatch marks filled the page, then concentrated in certain areas. When she squinted, they made a pattern, like five points.

He looked up into her deep blue eyes. She flushed at the intensity of his gaze.

"You see what I see, don't you?"

She pointed along the parchment. "It resembles the edges of a star. What do they represent?" she asked again.

"Anywhere we've had a run-in with a demon. I've suspected for a while that the attacks aren't random, but I don't know why. If I could figure out the pattern or purpose, Oceanea could sail again."

Lenora didn't know much about business, but she knew many of Oceanea's merchants relied on trade to support their families, and the poorest worked on fishing vessels. They had to be suffering now that the sirens had become more aggressive, and only the pirates were sailing.

She pointed to the center of the would-be star. "What's here?"

He shrugged. "The creatures or storms always pull us off course. I've tried more than once to sail that direction."

Lenora gasped. "That's it then, isn't it? Where they hide? Maybe it's their home."

He smiled, letting go of the edges of the paper. It curled up with a snap. "Thank you. I had a feeling you would be able to help me."

She flushed. "You're welcome." It was the closest thing to an explanation she'd been given for why he'd bothered to bring her on board. "I'd like to help you with more, you know, than swabbing the deck."

He pulled at his collar. "It's a rule amongst pirates. Newest recruit swabs the deck. I thought it'd help you fit in."

"Uh huh." She crossed her arms.

"Well, I'll take you off it. Time you learned some real skills. I could use another navigator and cartographer."

"Really?" She clapped her hands together.

Instead of answering, the captain pulled out several more pieces of parchment, showing her star charts he used in his calculations. "Sailing relies on careful planning and math, and a bit of drawing."

He pulled out a blank sheet, a quill, and a small jar of ink from one of his desk drawers. "Let me teach you."

Lenora held her hands up. "No, I couldn't waste your supplies."

Devonshire stood, giving her his chair. "I insist. I have plenty. I promise. We can get you your own set after the wind picks back up again, and we can return to shore."

"If you're sure." She slid into the vacated chair, and he leaned over her shoulder.

"First, you'll need to create a grid with a straight edge and decide the scale of your map."

Her father had taught her some mathematics, and she had learned drawing with a private tutor, but she was pleasantly surprised to find the work came easily and naturally to her.

Devonshire hummed his praise, filling her with warmth.

***

When a rap at the door interrupted her lesson hours later, Lenora was sad to see it end. The sails filled as the boat rode along on gentle waves. She nearly sagged in relief to see the ship moving again.

Instead of excusing himself, Devonshire brought her to the wheel of the ship. He grabbed her hands, putting them on the handles of the wheel. "A real sailor knows how to steer too. Which way is north?"

"That's easy." She smiled. "The sun rose over there, so we're pointed in the right direction."

"Aye, but what if it was cloudy?"

"I-I dunno. The stars?"

He fished something from his trouser pocket. "Clouds can cover the stars at night too, which is why we have this."

He handed her a small metal trinket. She thought it was a pocket watch at first, but it held only one hand, pointing at the N.

"It's called a compass. I got it from the goblins in my travels."

"Goblins?"

"Magical creatures residing in the Lumiara Mountains. They're collectors of all kinds of valuables – magical and otherwise."

Lenora squeezed the compass in her hand. Her heart sped up, thinking of her own dreams of travel. "When did you visit there?"

"After the war, before I took up sailing again."

"How does it work?"

"Magic, I think."

She ran her finger along the smooth surface of the glass. "I meant for sailing."

"The needle always points north, look." Devonshire took the tool, held his hand out, spinning around and darting from side to side.

Lenora watched the captain instead of the needle. "I think I need a second demonstration."

"What? Really." He came closer, handing it back to her. "Keep your eyes on the needle." He grabbed her other hand, dancing and spinning her. "Do you see?"

She laughed.

"Are you doing this to tease me, Lenora?" The captain's eyes met hers, and waves of warmth ran up and down her entire body.

"Maybe," she whispered, smiling. "I didn't know you could dance."

He smirked, drawing her into a sudden dip. She squealed. The smile on his face faltered, and he set her back on her feet.

"Keep the compass. I have more work I need to attend to."

He hurried back to his cabin, and Lenora stared after him, wondering what she'd done wrong.

Chapter Twelve
Knots

Lenora tapped at Loxi through the glass.

"Are you excited to be headed home?"

The salamander lifted its arms, expressing his ambivalence.

"Well, I am. I can't wait to step foot on dry land again." Her heart sped up. She wasn't sure how long they'd stop, but if Lord Darlington paid the captain to keep Oceanea safe, she assumed she'd have a chance to see her father. She wanted to ask the captain directly about it, but she hadn't had a chance to speak to him since he stormed off yesterday.

She exhaled. Despite his distant behavior, she was eager for the most inconsequential and minuscule moments.

Early this morning, she knocked at his cabin, meaning to invite him to join her for breakfast, but he outright ignored her, not meeting her gaze as she bored down on him through the windows dotting the outside of his private quarters. Yet other times, his eyes followed her as she mopped or walked by his cabin. If she turned his direction, he'd busy himself or storm off.

It was infuriating. Why did he run so hot and cold?

She stretched back out on her bed, intending to go back to sleep, when the rocking of the ship intensified. She started for the door when Loxi slapped at the sides of his tank, asking to come with her, but she ignored it.

"You'll be safer here," she said, clicking the door shut and refusing to meet the axolotl's wordless displeasure.

The men ran up the stairs, scrambling to their places. As she emerged into the open air, the musty odor of the unwashed men from the underbelly of the ship gave way to the fresh, salty air.

By the time she made it to the deck, most of the crew had harpoons in hand.

Another attack.

Knowing the captain plotted their course to seek the creatures out, she hadn't expected another on their way back home.

Devonshire stood at the helm, barking orders and holding a trident. The wind whipped his long hair and clothing. Her heart tripled at the sight of him, but he didn't glance in her direction. His beard had grown in the last couple of weeks, but she found she didn't mind it, nor did she mind his tanned skin any longer. What once spoke to her of the villainy of pirating life reminded her of his brave sacrifice to his country. He was a hero.

She clutched her weapon but kept her eyes on the captain instead of the water.

What was happening to her?

The boat bumped, knocking Lenora flat against the deck. She groaned. Devonshire hovered above her in an instant, pulling her back to her feet. "I need you."

Her face heated as he guided her to the wheel of the ship. She rolled her eyes when she caught his meaning.

"Do you still have the compass I gave you?"

"Of course." Last night she held it while she slept.

She grabbed it from the pocket of her dress, handing it over to him. He closed her fingers around it. "Use it to keep us on course."

"B-but –"

"I'm trusting you, Lenora. You're more than capable, and you'll be safer here than near the water's edge."

She swallowed and nodded.

The ship bobbed, lifting and jerking. Keeping north proved more difficult than Lenora had imagined. Her fingers and arms trembled, holding the wheel in place. Mopping the deck had provided her with some grip strength, but she found steering during an attack was a new level of effort she was unaccustomed to.

The wheel jerked her to the side, and she leaned all her weight against it.

Splashes started washing over the deck, and Lenora's stomach tightened. She pulled her ear coverings from her pocket – now a permanent accessory with every new outfit.

She caught sight of the towering form and gasped. Its ocean blue eyes and pale square jaw were framed with short jet black hair, matching the coloring of the previous sirens, but it was a male. She didn't realize that was possible, though now that she thought about it, how had she thought these creatures existed without males?

Her stomach knotted as she held tight to the wheel, but the waves were already calming and the ship leveled. The effort of wrapping the material tightly around her ears proved unnecessary. Had the siren fled? Or had the men already killed it?

Lenora released her throbbing fingers from the wheel, shaking her arms out.

Devonshire strode back over to her, drenched head-to-toe with a wide smile on his face. He untied her hastily attached stockings. She warmed at the caring, familiar gesture. Once he had one ear uncovered, he announced, "Quickest victory yet!"

"Great job." She squeezed his hand, emboldened by his tender attention.

"I feel like celebrating. Will you meet me out here later?"

"Here?"

"On the deck. After everyone but the night crew retires."

She smiled. "Of course."

"I'll take over steering. See if you can track down Percy and have him show you how to knot the sails."

She bit her lip as an unbidden wave of grief rolled over her. "Leopold was teaching me knots before he died."

The captain's warm, brown eyes appraised her. "Of course, he was a kind, young man. I'm sorry he's gone."

She nodded, not trusting herself to speak.

He leaned toward her, hesitating for a moment, before gathering her hand into his. Turning it over, he examined her reddened palm. "You did a great job at the wheel today."

"Thank you."

Devonshire stared for a second more before raising it to his lips. They barely brushed her skin, but a spark of heat traveled up her arm.

He released her hand slowly, and she leaned closer to him. "What was that for?" she asked, breathlessly.

"A thank you for being here, for helping steer the ship."

Percy called over to them. "Whatcha doin' over there, making an old man wait, huh?"

Devonshire cringed, laughing. "Sorry. Probably shouldn't have asked Percy first. I told him he's your new teacher, and he's an impatient grump."

***

Walking in a daze, Lenora rubbed her thumb over the spot of the kiss, replaying the moment over and over.

Percy, as predicted, tapped his foot with an air of great displeasure. "You took long enough."

She curtseyed, refusing to let the old pirate ruffle her feathers. "I'm pleased the captain trusts me to learn such an important job."

Percy laughed. "This grunt work? When he lets you help with his secret maps, then tell me about his trust."

Her lips parted. "He has."

Percy's eyes widened before he let out a long whistle. She relished his surprise until he added, "So we can expect little Devonshires soon?"

Her face turned the shade of a tomato, and the old man chuckled again.

"Here I'll show you how to tie and loosen the sails."

Thankful for the change in subject, she studied the man's agile fingers. It wasn't till she looked up at the sails that she noticed a fabric lump several yards away on the deck.

"What's that?"

The man quirked his furry brow. "The siren."

"Why is he still there?"

"It, you mean, and we're all filled up at the moment. Hopefully, we'll make it to shore before it starts stinking."

Lenora wrinkled her nose and repressed the impulse to gag.

"Sorry, not an appropriate conversation topic for a lady."

"No, it's fine… Are the bodies of the sirens we hunt stored in the unmarked room downstairs?"

"Aye."

"Why is it locked?"

"Why yer pokin' 'round?"

"I…" her face heated. "I was curious, just searching around my new home. I was surprised when I found the locked door."

Percy frowned, untying the mess of rope she'd made, demonstrating a second time before untying and handing it back to her. "I've put a few bodies of friends and foes down there in my months aboard, and it's never been locked before. I imagine the captain may have done it to protect yer delicate sensibilities."

She nodded, testing and looping the rope. What Percy said made sense. Why had she been so curious? She glanced at the covered form of the siren.

"Do you think it'd be okay for me to look at it?"

Percy yanked the rope from her hand, rubbing at her already sore palm.

"Ah!" she sucked in a sharp breath.

"Concentrate, woman!"

"Sorry."

Hours later, Lenora's fingers felt raw from yanking at the coils of rope. She dragged herself back downstairs, intending to wash for her late-night meeting with the captain, but threw herself down on her bed for a moment of rest first.

She never managed a straight answer from Percy, and she wasn't bold enough to walk off and pull the tarp away from the body of the siren with him watching.

But if she hurried, she might beat the captain.

Chapter Thirteen
Knots

When she came out on the deck, she noticed immediately that the body had been moved. She stared at the spot it had been, considering her options with an unnerving wave of disappointment. Her heels clacked along the wooden surface, overly loud along the empty deck, as she searched for signs of the siren. She clenched her gloved fingers, swishing the skirts of her sky-blue satin gown.

She'd selected the most elegant, clean outfit she could find, securing it with a yellow sash from another dress and hoping the captain didn't notice the row of open buttons along the back. Without the help of a lady's maid, she'd avoided wearing her finer frocks, but she wanted to look her best tonight.

She tapped her toe. She'd moved to the spot she'd seen the siren earlier, but there was nothing. If the locked room below deck was full, like Percy suggested, where could it have been stashed?

"I hope you haven't been waiting too long." Devonshire's deep voice made her jump.

"No."

He bowed, and she took his extended hand. He was wearing the suit from their engagement ceremony, but unlike before, she admired how handsome he looked.

"You clean up nicely."

He smiled. "I would say as do you, but you always look nice to me."

Heat crept up her neck, from the unexpected compliment, and she swallowed. They were standing inches from one another.

A screech of a violin rang out, and Lenora threw her arms around the captain.

Percy stood a few feet away, holding the instrument. "Sorry, I'm a little rusty. Let me try again."

She cringed as a few more sharp notes pierced the air until Percy had the strings vibrating smoothly.

Devonshire laughed. "I asked Percy to play for us. We never got a chance to dance at the party."

"I'm sorry. I was –"

"Frightened, revolted, devastated?"

She gave a shrill, nervous laugh, trying to decide if she should lie.

He led her along the deck, turning her on her heels and leading her in a dance. She recognized the footwork, and the captain's graceful movements were as fine as any gentleman's she had ever partnered with. Her heart thrummed, enjoying the closeness and the feel of her hands in his.

She looked up into Devonshire's kind brown eyes, crinkled at the corners from too much sun, and answered his previous question, even though several minutes had passed. "I was upset about our engagement, but that was before we knew each other."

"Thank you for your honesty. So then, what do you think of me now?"

She swallowed. "I think you're a great captain: brave and clever."

"What about as your fiancé?"

"Today you're doing quite well."

"But not at first?" He raised his brows.

"No," she admitted. "You weren't around me at all. I hardly understood why you wanted to get engaged."

Something flickered over his face, and Lenora regretted her words instantly. "I mean, uh…"

"You don't have to apologize. You're being honest."

She lowered her face. He slid his hand under her chin, tipping it up toward his own.

"I want you to be yourself with me. I kept my distance because I wanted you to get comfortable. I didn't want you to feel obligated to me, not when you were forced into the engagement."

She was breathless and dizzy. Her lips were inches from Devonshire's.

The music stopped. Percy cleared his throat. "This is getting mighty awkward. I'll just be excusin' meself."

Lenora leapt away from the captain, covering her burning face, and Percy chuckled. She'd nearly forgotten about the old pirate. *How embarrassing.*

"Maybe no music is better." Devonshire rubbed at the back of his neck. "Though I'm hoping the new crew members will be musical. We used to have more that could play."

"New crew?"

His face fell. "To replace the men that died."

"Oh."

The silence stretched on.

Lenora regretted the moment they'd lost and searched for a change in subject. "How many days will we be on shore, do you think?"

Devonshire stepped away from her, frowning. "Not days, Lenora, hours, and you will be staying on board."

"What?" she asked more loudly than she intended, and then in a more natural volume she added, "Why?"

He crossed his arms. "I think you know."

"I do not," she insisted.

"I can't have you running away."

"Excuse me?"

"Are you telling me that if I let you return home, you'd come back to the ship?"

"Of course!"

He raised an eyebrow and tilted his head as if to say he didn't believe her.

"How dare you?" she spat. "You commanded me on this ship without any explanation, and now you hold me captive?"

The furrow in his brow deepened. "I did nothing of the sort. I made an arrangement with your father, and you came willingly, did you not?" His voice rose.

"What other choice did I have? I'd been forced to get engaged to a stranger and dropped off at his ship –"

"And you ask me why I've kept my distance? Were your words from before empty flattery? I do not wish to force you to do anything. I thought you understood."

His words hung in the air. A cool breeze made her shiver. She wouldn't apologize, not when he refused to let her off the ship.

Devonshire snapped. "Go back to your quarters. You'll be warmer there."

"At least let me see my father," she pleaded.

"I'm sorry," Devonshire said, and she could see that he truly was. "Your father sends a liaison of the Sea Farers to pay us and collect the monsters. We won't be seeing him."

Tears started, and she did as the captain had instructed. She went back to her quarters.

***

She heard the stomping of feet along the deck and the shouts of joy. They'd landed.

But Lenora wouldn't be joining them.

She sobbed into her pillow. What was the point? So she could see her former country, but not step on shore?

Why had her father approved of this life for his only child?

Her pillow was soaked, and she reached into her pocket for a handkerchief, but she found the captain's compass instead.

She gritted her teeth. Without thinking, she chucked the gift at the wall. It smacked against the wood with a crash, and she sucked in her breath.

What have I done?

Worry churned in her stomach as she leapt from her bed to inspect the magical tool. Shattered glass covered her floor. Loxi hovered near the side of the tank, watching her. Lenora held her breath as she turned the metal casing over. The needle had popped off.

No, no!

With trembling fingers, she searched the floorboards until she found the tiny needle. She nearly slumped in relief. Pressing the needle back into place, she jabbed her finger against a remaining shard of glass.

"Ah!" She sucked on the bleeding appendage before turning the compass around and around. The needle turned, not settling on north, but swaying with each jerky movement.

She'd broken it.

It was clear that whatever magic had made it work was useless now.

A knock on her door made her jump. Exchanging a guilty look with her axolotl, she shoved the compass back into her pocket.

"Come on, Nora," Percy's voice sounded through the door.

The unexpected use of her childhood nickname had her on her feet. "Yes?"

"Open up."

She cracked the door an inch.

"Why're ya stayin' cooped up in here when you could stretch your legs on the shore?"

"The captain won't let me," she sniffled.

"Phooey." Percy pushed her door open and grabbed her hand. "I'll put myself in charge of you, okay?"

"Really?"

"Of course, I can't stand to let a woman cry."

Chapter Fourteen
Back in Oceanea

Lenora greatly underestimated how much she missed standing on ground that didn't move. The dusty dirt, soft grass, and green trees made her heart soar with nostalgic pleasure.

Walking along the docks with Percy, she pulled leaves and flowers from trees, making herself a crown, like she'd done as a young girl.

The old man patted her hand affectionately. "Told ya, a walk about is just what ya spirit needed."

"Thank you, Percy."

The sailors mostly milled about, but some headed to town. Lenora didn't see Captain Devonshire and assumed he'd been one of the first to disembark. She told herself she didn't care.

Percy led her further from the docks. "There's a merchant and a pub. Nothing else for miles, and these two have ta keep rebuildin.' Suppose the business they get from desperate sailors makes it worthwhile."

"Because of the sirens?"

"Aye. You've seen the size of 'em now. They send giant waves over the shore. The fact that these businesses are here now shows we've been doin' a mighty good job."

Lenora smiled despite herself. She was part of that effort now.

The fishy-smelling mercantile was hardly bigger than her private quarters on board the ship. The rustic little building used every square inch efficiently. Baskets hung from the ceiling, and shelves lined the walls, crammed with flour, sugar, bolts of fabric, rope, and every manner of supplies. Despite the shop's size, one could spend hours searching every corner. Next to the small register was a rack of pale colored bonnets.

Lenora slid the captain's hat from her head. "I'd like to get a lady's hat, so I can return the captain's."

Percy jingled his pocket. "All I ever buy on shore is alcohol. I've got more gold than I could ever spend… well, should. Let me get ya something."

"Thank you."

She selected a buttery-yellow one stitched with eyelets of flowers that she thought would weather. Tying the ribbon under her chin, she studied herself in the mirror. The bonnet contrasted nicely with her dark hair and wouldn't be as hot as the captain's sturdy navy three-cornered hat.

Percy paid before dragging her to the pub next door.

The pub was open-air, missing walls and framed by four wooden posts, covered with a roof made from a patchwork of old, tattered sails. Small tables and chairs crammed underneath, shaded from the summer sun. A single employee stood next to crates of clean and dirty glassware. There was no bar, only barrels of ale served into the clean pints. A line snaked from the pub's single employee all the way back to their ship.

Lenora relaxed in a seat facing the land and fanned herself. Percy plunked a large glass in front of her.

"No, thank you."

He winked. "Both are for me."

She snorted. "Okay then. I thought you said you had a hard time spending all your gold?"

He laughed. "How much do you think a drink costs? We sometimes don't return for months. I think I'm safe."

Lenora relaxed, watching the smiling crew of men around her. She was glad she'd disobeyed the captain. Percy's easy grin slid off his face, and Lenora's heart quickened, suspecting what the sudden change meant.

"I thought I told you not to leave the ship," Devonshire's deep voice growled from behind her.

Lenora tried to keep her voice steady as she craned her neck and retorted, "I only went here and the mercantile."

Devonshire gripped her arm, lifting her from her seat, and addressing Percy, "You're fired."

The old man shrugged, taking a long sip, as if disinterested in his employment, but Lenora was outraged. "He did nothing wrong!"

"He disobeyed my direct order."

"I didn't tell him," she lied.

Devonshire leaned toward her. "I told them. I told all of them. Percy was supposed to keep an eye on you on the ship."

"Oh," she swallowed. "Still, I talked him into it, and no harm's been done."

"You're wrong," he snapped. "You're coming with me, and Percy is fired."

Tears started, and Lenora swiped at them quickly. The crowded pub had grown quiet, observing the squabble. It didn't help that they were mostly from their same ship.

Percy called over to her as she was being led away. "Don't worry about me, Miss! There's plenty of ships that would love an old, experienced pirate like me."

"He's right," Devonshire mumbled. "It's a pity to lose him."

"Then why –"

"He disobeyed my orders."

She wrenched her arm loose from his grip. "And are you so full of pride that an old man attempting to be kind to your fiancé deserves this kind of punishment?"

He grumbled something indecipherable as they made the short journey back.

"No." She crossed her arms, refusing to take another step toward the ship. "I will not go aboard until you answer my questions."

Devonshire blew out a breath between gritted teeth. She took that as a sign of her victory.

Lifting her chin, she forced herself to ask, "Why do you treat me like this? One moment you're affectionate and charming, the next you're as cold as the snow on Thornveil Isle."

"Thornveil Isle?" Devonshire's brow furrowed. "That's very far from here. How do you know about the vampires' country?"

"I had the best private tutor my father's money could buy. Now answer the question!" she snapped.

Gulls cried overhead, filling the tense silence. Lenora breathed heavily with her fists clutched at her sides. If the captain refused her now, she would throw him into the ocean.

He shook his head. "No, Lenora. How about you explain to me why you disobeyed my orders?"

"I missed the land. Is this the sort of man you are, making demands of your betrothed like some common pirate?"

"If she's as stubborn as you, then yes."

Grunting, Lenora shoved the captain toward the water.

But he didn't move.

She tried again, ramming her shoulder into his chest with all her weight thrown behind it. Devonshire's eyes widened, and he started to laugh.

Turning back to the ship, she stormed across the gangplank. The captain's laughter rang in her ears. She was so angry that she forgot to be afraid.

***

Lenora stomped all the way below deck, fetching a feeder fish from the storage closet for Loxi before locking herself in her bedroom for the rest of the day. The barrel brimmed with small fish, and the rest of the room was stocked with fresh supplies. She supposed this meant the captain had plans to be away from land for longer. She groaned.

When she went to toss the fish into Loxi's tank, she noticed it was different – larger with colorful rocks lining the bottom and a peony-pink coral arch. Loxi paused momentarily to gobble the fish before darting in and around his new tank decoration.

She stared at him through the glass, sniffling. "The captain fired Percy, Loxi."

The salamander swam in circles. If he understood what she was talking about this time, he showed no sign. Sighing, she stared in the direction of her half-empty trunk and growing pile of dirty gowns. Except they were gone.

She opened the trunk. Her previous garments had been replaced with lighter frocks, ones without fasteners that she could slide over her head. A stack of bonnets, much like the one she'd purchased, and a sachet of dried flowers were neatly folded inside. Next to the trunk were soft leather shoes that looked much more inviting than the stiff heels she wore.

She hugged her arms around herself.

The captain had done all this for her, and she'd yelled at him. Although he'd deserved it, a lump formed in her throat. Things had been going so well between them.

"What should I do, Loxi? He fired Percy and tried to force me to stay aboard."

The axolotl didn't even glance in her direction.

"Maybe he wanted me to be here for this surprise?" She tapped her foot against her bedframe. Why had she listened to Percy? She'd ruined an opportunity to receive these thoughtful gifts from the captain. She'd been feeling sorry for herself, and although she didn't agree with the firing, she supposed Devonshire had a point. He needed men who would follow his orders.

But she also needed a husband who would listen to her.

Her time on land was more necessary than any gift. Perhaps if she talked to Devonshire, she could make him understand. Did he realize how terribly frightening it was for her to be uprooted from her life and basically imprisoned on this ship? She had come to care for him, but she wasn't certain he understood her predicament or her feelings.

She made her way to the deck. Most of the crew had returned, and she recognized the preparation for cast off. The captain wasn't at the helm, so she checked his cabin. As always, he'd locked himself in, but she could see him through the windows.

She knocked before proceeding to tap on the windows and yell, "Captain, open up! I can see you."

He shook his head and got up from his desk. He opened the door a crack. "Most of the crew know better than to pester me like this."

"But I'm not part of your crew."

He sighed. "I suppose not."

"I wanted to thank you for the lovely gifts – for the tank and the clothes. It was really thoughtful, and I'm sorry I wasn't here to receive it."

His frown flickered for a moment, encouraging her.

"I think I understand why you wanted me to stay on the ship –"

"No, you don't."

His interruption cleared her brain of her pre-planned speech. "What do you mean?"

"Why do you think you're here, Lenora?"

She swallowed, her cheeks heating. His diary's words came back to her, but she wasn't sure it was wise to admit she'd snooped in his things. She decided on the truth. "You want companionship."

He gestured along the deck. "I have plenty."

She grabbed his hand. "It's different, and you know it."

He pulled it away, shaking his head. "I never should've spent time with you. It's only muddled things…"

"Whatever do you mean?" Her eyes widened. What was wrong with a betrothed couple spending time together?

Instead of answering, he led her from the room, shutting the door in her face.

Chapter Fifteen
The Storm

Since the captain hadn't emerged from his cabin, Lenora went to the helm as the sails pulled the ship from the harbor. The gusts were strong enough that the ship would quickly be brought off course without someone steering. Had the captain known she'd do it?

The strange events of the last few days were an unsolvable puzzle. The captain had warmed to her, spending time with her to teach her about sailing. He'd apologized for the frightening and sudden engagement ceremony, implying that's why he'd kept his initial distance. She'd seen his innermost thoughts in his journal, where he'd longed for companionship. He'd shown her his secret charts, asking for her advice, and he'd planned a romantic evening and given her gifts.

She bit her lip, trying to stem her fresh tears.

It would've been better if he'd remained distant and cold like when she'd first arrived.

Hours passed, and the wind picked up. Without instruction, she steered south, but she knew the captain had plotted a course that he'd yet to share with her and the crew.

When he came out of the cabin, relief washed over her. He headed straight for her. Surely, he would acknowledge his thoughtlessness and explain himself. His furrowed brow and frown showed his displeasure.

"Move, Lenora," he said, as thunder boomed in the distance.

She gasped. "I thought you came to apologize." The wind blew her hair into her eyes and flapped her skirts.

"Thank you for guiding the ship. Now let me take over."

"What would you like me to –"

He cut her off, his words full of acid. "Whatever you want, Lenora. Please stop pestering me. In fact, next time we go to shore. You can stay."

His words were the cold slap of reality. Every muscle in her body tensed.

She wasn't going to try with this difficult, arrogant man any longer. Storming away, she intended to make herself useful with the sails, but the men just shooed her away like an annoyance. A light sprinkling of rain made her shiver.

She missed Percy and Leopold. If she'd ever felt loneliness before in her life, it was nothing compared to this. Stuck on a ship without a purpose, a distant fiancé, and perpetually friendless. Why was she here? Did Devonshire truly want to marry her? Did he want a wife?

He behaved as if he needed no one, least of all her.

She gritted her teeth, intending to turn back to the helm and give the captain a piece of her mind, but the gusting wind and rain made it difficult. Clouds darkened overhead. Thunder clapped again, louder this time, giving her pause. Rain poured, obscuring her vision and soaking her through.

Her anger cooled, replaced by fear. She hadn't experienced any bad weather at sea and wasn't sure how to plan for it.

The wind blew harder, sending crashing waves higher and higher along the sides of the boat. Lightning cracked in the distance. Her heart pounded. This storm seemed dangerous for sailing. Had she steered them right into it? Why hadn't the captain changed course?

"Lenora!" Devonshire yelled in the wind. It was little more than a whisper over the din of the storm. Pulling up her soaked skirts and squinting, she ran back to the wheel of the ship and the captain. "I need the compass."

"I…" Dread filled her. With everything that had transpired, she hadn't had a chance to confess.

Another flicker of lightning and booming thunder made her squeal.

"Lenora! Now! The ship has shifted. I'll need it to keep on course."

Through the pelting rain, she fished it from her pocket without explanation and pressed it into the captain's hand.

Hurt flickered over his face before it contorted in anger. He tapped at the useless needle, attempting to reignite its lost magic. Eventually, he lifted his eyes back to hers, and the air went out of her.

"What did you do?" he shouted.

"It was an accident."

"I trusted you, Lenora, with something invaluable. If we're blown off course, it might be weeks till we sort it out. You've put our lives in danger."

"I'm sorry." She choked back a sob, feeling ashamed and foolish. What kind of child throws something so important in a fit of passion?

"Leave me." He lifted his arm, turning back to the wheel and refusing to meet her gaze. It was somehow worse than being yelled at.

Lenora intended to go below deck, but the ship bounced dangerously from side to side as the waves and wind whipped.

A sail came loose from its rope, and Lenora scrambled to help secure it. It took three of them to tie it down. The rain and sky howled, and the sails flapped back and forth as if the storm couldn't make up its mind. Lenora clung to the mast as the stern of the ship rose dangerously higher with each cresting wave.

Her pulse roared in her ears. This was different and more deadly than even the attacks with the sirens. There was nothing the sailors could do to calm the churning waters but ride out the storm and wait.

Lenora squeezed her eyes shut, praying to the Maker. They flew open again as her feet gave way on the slick surface beneath her, and she lost her grip on the mast, sliding helplessly along the deck. The ship was tipped almost ninety degrees in the air. Lighting flashed in the sky, hitting the mast with an explosion of light and sound. It cracked down the middle, and the sails were aflame.

Lenora cried out as she tumbled down the length of the ship.

Devonshire caught her, his own arms looped in the rungs of the wheel. He kissed her, so quickly she thought she imagined it. Their eyes locked, and he ran his thumb along her jawline. He mouthed a lengthy explanation she couldn't hear, but it meant everything.

The wind screamed. The intensity of the storm made it impossible to speak, to say the things unsaid. Lenora wrapped her arms tighter around the captain, burying her face in his chest when the ship rolled, throwing them into the deep, black water and drowning out every thought.

***

Lenora blinked awake. Her heart pounded, and her muscles ached. She groaned. She was soaked head to toe. Memory of the storm came back to her as she sat up.

Where was she?

She looked up, but where the sky should be was arching gray stone. Stalactites hung from the ceiling, dripping with streams of water. In the dull light, she could see nothing but rock.

She sucked in a breath of the damp air. Where was everyone? There was no water inside the cavern, so that ruled out the possibility she'd washed up here.

Pulling herself from her rocky bed with a groan, she swayed on her feet, and blackness threatened to pull her under again. The space was empty and quiet except for the constant drip, drip, drip of the ceiling.

She squeezed her eyes shut for a moment, leaning against the rock where she'd been lying. Her hand brushed a silken pillow. The surface of the rock was smooth, like it had been worn away for just this purpose. Her hand went to her brow, noticing for the first time a bandage wrapped around it.

She wasn't alone then.

"You're awake," a voice sounded from behind her, and Lenora shrieked.

She spun, nearly collapsing from the shift in her weight.

A woman roughly the same age as Lenora, with waist-length black hair, pale skin, and deep blue eyes, wore a gown of what appeared to be knotted seaweed. "I didn't mean to startle you."

Lenora gasped. "Where am I?" The question echoed in her brain, causing her to wince. The woman was eerily familiar, but Lenora's head hurt so much, it was hard to think clearly.

The woman spoke in a whisper, "You've had a head injury. Don't worry. You are safe with us, Daughter."

Lenora's pounding head muddled her thinking. *Daughter?*

The woman stepped closer, cupping Lenora's face with her hands. "Don't you recognize me?"

Lenora blinked. The wide eyes, the nearly translucent skin, the warm smile. Her stomach lurched, and she whispered, "You're a siren." She tried to pull away, but the woman held her firmly.

"I'm your mother."

"My mother?" Lenora's memories were murky. She remembered her dark hair, but everything else was hazy. Her aching head made it hard to ask any questions. Her mother wasn't a siren. She was dead.

"Yes."

"But… but…"

"Shh, there will be time for answers. Right now, you need to rest."

Lenora allowed herself to be guided back to her bed of rock, closing her eyes immediately. The woman hummed a melody.

Lenora tensed, thinking of the sirens luring the sailors to their deaths, and tried to fight the song's effects, but either the woman's magic was too powerful or her injuries were too great. The melody wrapped itself around Lenora's body, filling her with a soothing hum. Lenora was brought back to her early childhood, when her mother was still alive, and she drifted off.

Chapter Sixteen
The Cavern

When Lenora awoke the second time, her head no longer hurt. Still, it was difficult to make sense of everything that had happened. She knew they'd crashed, but she didn't know if anyone else had survived. The thought churned in her stomach, filling her with worry. She fingered her pearl earrings, thinking of Captain Devonshire's warm, strong arms around her, and the words unsaid between them.

Had Loxi survived? She thought her axolotl would have better luck than the crew, but what if he was unable to escape his tank? If it cracked during the crash, perhaps he could survive, but she wasn't sure about the salt water. He was just a pet, but he'd been with her for most of her life. She didn't feel complete without him.

The other thing she couldn't make sense of, as hard as she tried, was how she ended up in this strange, stony cavern with a siren claiming to be her dead mother. Was the woman telling the truth? Why would she save Lenora? Maybe the woman wasn't a siren but just happened to look like one of them?

Based on the effects of her song, Lenora wasn't ready to believe that.

Head throbbing, she blinked at the unchanging cave ceiling. The tattered, stiff fabric of her gown rubbed against her legs, but other than her head, she seemed to be uninjured.

The woman couldn't really be her mother, could she? Her raven hair matched Lenora's memory, but she was far too young, and they were in the middle of the ocean. Lenora remembered her mother's sickness, the morning father had broken the news, and the funeral they'd held several days later.

He wouldn't have lied to her.

Lenora swung her feet over the side of the rocky platform, running her hand along the pink satin pillow. A memory pinched in her brain, snuggling up beside Mother after a bad dream, her pink pillow…

She gasped, pulling her hand to her trembling mouth. What did it mean? Her stomach twisted again.

The drip of the stalactites continued, and her stomach grumbled. Her mouth and throat were painfully dry. She wasn't ready to trust the woman yet, but she had no other option but to look for her. She wove through the cavern in the direction she'd seen the woman come and go. The cave narrowed around her, resembling a long hallway running in two directions. Soft twinkling lights glowed in a domed netting above her. She touched the rough surface, determining it was seaweed. She wasn't sure what magic made it glow, but it reminded her of the boards in the ship and of starlight.

She paused, looking down both stretches of hallway.

Maybe this was a bad idea.

Lenora didn't know which way to go, and there could be other people here who wouldn't appreciate her snooping. She waited. Her stomach grumbled louder, and she licked her dried, cracked lips. She needed food and water.

Turning to the right, her feet padded slowly forward against the cold stone surface – she must've lost her new shoes in the crash. Heart pounding, she held her breath. Why was she on edge? If the siren woman had wanted to hurt her, she'd had plenty of opportunity, but a gnawing of uncertainty made Lenora hesitate.

What could a sea monster possibly want with Lenora? If this woman was her mother, why had Father told Lenora she died? And if she'd been alive these last eleven years, why had she never come looking for her daughter?

Lenora didn't understand any of it.

The stony hallway split in two. She went to the right again. The hall dead-ended into an open cavern, much like the one she'd come from. Turning, she backtracked to the second fork. This hall twisted, and Lenora feared she might not find its end when she heard the murmuring of voices.

She ran, finding a wooden door fitted in place of the arching stone opening. She tried the knob. It was locked.

Before she thought the better of it, she pounded on the door. "Hello?"

A cacophony of men's voices rose, and then hushed.

Captain Devonshire's low, bellowing voice sounded raspy, "Lenora, is that you?"

"Captain!" she cried. "I thought I was the only survivor."

"Can you get us out of here?"

She jiggled the handle again, throwing her entire weight into her shoulder, but the door didn't move. "I-I'll need to find the key."

"The cells are locked too."

"Cells?" Lenora's head spun.

"Yes, the demon's captured us. How did you get free?"

"I didn't. She said…" Lenora's chin wobbled. She couldn't make herself say it.

"Are you safe?"

She let the captain's voice steady her, and she let out a loud exhale. "Yes, I think so."

"Good." She could feel the smile behind his words. "Do what you can, Lenora, but don't sacrifice yourself for us."

"Captain…"

"Promise me."

She ran her hand along the wooden door, longing to see the captain's face. "Alright. I promise."

***

Lenora's heart went into her throat as she tiptoed back to her room. She had wanted to stay near the captain, to ask what he had told her before the crash and confess her own feelings, but she needed to free him and the others. What would happen if she ran into the creature claiming to be her mother? Any possibility that this woman wasn't a siren was gone. She had captured the captain and the crew.

Lenora had never been good at lying. She considered whether she should search the other end of the hall, but her body was trembling. She needed to find the keys and free the men, but she didn't want to run into the siren when her nerves were so frayed. Lying back down on the rocky bed, she patted her cool hands on her flushed face, letting the dripping sounds of the cave steady her.

When her breathing slowed, she pushed to her feet. She shook out her arms, staring at the open doorway. Should she risk it? She couldn't very well pretend her betrothed and his crew of men weren't locked away down the hall. She walked to the doorway, intending to search the other hall for clues and fumbling for an alibi if she was discovered.

Before she left the room, the siren woman stepped inside, balancing a breakfast tray. "Lenora! You're up! How's your head?"

Lenora's hands went back up to her bandaged forehead. "Better, I think. You know my name?"

The woman trilled. "Of course I do, you're my daughter. I named you Lenora because you were born in the light, instead of in the darkness of the sea."

Lenora blinked again, studying the woman's deep blue eyes.

Her voice took on a softer quality. "Don't you remember me?"

"I'm not sure…" Lenora's chest tightened with raw emotion. She'd give anything to see her mother again, but she couldn't trust her. "You look too young to be my mother."

She smiled. "That's because I'm a siren. We don't age like humans." She lifted the tray. "You must be starving."

She walked past Lenora, plunking down the tray on the rocky bed. "Come on, Lenora."

Lenora's mind recalled a memory of her mother running along the shore, calling out to her in the shallows. *"Come on, Lenora."* If this wasn't her, she could be her twin. Even her voice sounded the same as Lenora's memory. She backed away. If this was really her mother, then… then…

The woman patted the rock. "What're you doing? Come join me. I'm sure you have a lot of questions."

Lenora's knees weakened, and she collapsed.

"Lenora!" The woman bolted to her side. Her eyes wide with concern. "Are you alright?"

Lenora sniffled, shaking out her dark hair that was the same raven color as this woman's. As the siren's.

"What's the matter?" Her mother brushed the hair from her eyes.

"I remember you."

She smiled, her white teeth looked sharp, and Lenora recoiled as the woman threw her arms around her. "You're home. My daughter is finally home."

Chapter Seventeen
Questions

Instead of talking, Lenora downed her cup of water before starting on her grilled fish. Her mother took the glass and came back with another. This time Lenora drank slower. She felt steadier, and her mind was clearer, but the looming reality of her situation made her feel buried.

The captive crew tugged at her mind in a constant rhythm that matched the dripping cave. Drip, drip, drip. *Monster, monster, monster.*

Her mother stared at her, but Lenora couldn't meet her eyes. She searched for something to say. "Is this your home?"

"Yes, I've lived here the past eleven years." Since she'd left Lenora and her father.

Lenora forced herself to exhale. "Where are we exactly?"

"Under the water in an open-air cavern. I found you after the boat crash and brought you back here." Her mother scooped up her hands into her own. She looked unnaturally young, not a day over twenty-five.

"How…" She wasn't sure what to start with. How had she saved her? How had she been able to see the crash?

Why did she leave Lenora and her father? Lenora curled and uncurled her fingers.

"Ask it."

Lenora took another sip of water, deciding on how to phrase her question. "Am I a siren?"

"Part-siren, yes."

She'd already pieced it together, but the truth churned in her gut. "Does Father know?" She forced herself to meet her mother's eyes, hoping for the truth.

She nodded. "Yes."

Lenora's mouth went dry. Her mother was a monster, and her father was a liar. She tasted bile in her throat and willed herself to continue, but the bitterness burned through her soul as well as her gut.

Perhaps this is why the Maker never answered her prayers.

Lenora was a monster, a demon, according to Devonshire. It was hard to think clearly enough to ask more questions. How had her parents ended up together?

She traced the rock with her finger, trying to calm her grated nerves. "It's lucky you were able to find me."

"Sirens can feel each other's presence. I could sense you calling me."

Lenora bit her lip, drawing blood. She didn't want any connection to this woman.

Her mother continued, "I'd been searching the ocean, awaiting your return for months. Your father promised he would return you to the ocean by your eighteenth birthday. Apparently, he thought he could double-cross me by giving you to those bloodthirsty pirates."

Before she could think better of it, Lenora said, "They're not…"

"The pirates? They hunt our kind from the ocean. We used to live on islands, now we're forced into underwater caverns or at the tops of high cliffs."

"That isn't true," Lenora countered. "The sailors have sought out the sirens because they attack ships, even homes along the coast."

Her mother shook out her long black hair, and she was struck with the image of the black snaking tendrils, grabbing men from the deck of the ship.

Acid filled her mouth again. She knew it wasn't wise, knew she should choose her words carefully, but anger, disgust, and betrayal won. Lenora spat, "You're a monster!"

Her mother's eyes widened, and her voice cracked. "No, Lenora! We only seek to protect ourselves. Have some of our people become too bold, going on the offensive? Maybe. But most of us spend our days in hiding. If we're so monstrous, how do you think you came to be?"

Our people.

Lenora rubbed her arms, willing the sudden chill away.

Her mother continued, "No doubt the pirates were attempting to use you as a token."

Lenora's heart sped into a gallop. "What do you mean, 'token?'"

"The pirates discovered long ago that sirens can't sink ships with other living sirens onboard."

She touched her earrings, twisting them in her fingers. Was this why the captain had brought her on board? Her stomach clenched, and she thought she might be sick. His behavior had been so strange and inconsistent. She remembered him asking her, *"Why do you think you're here, Lenora?"*

Her mother seemed to read her mind. "Did he ever force you to stay on the ship?"

"Y-yes."

She sighed. "That's part myth, but some believe the magic breaks if the siren leaves, even for a moment."

If her father had known the truth, perhaps so had Devonshire. The arrangement with her father, the captain's distant behavior, his refusal to let her leave… everything clicked into place.

Clenching her jaw to hold back the stream of tears, she forced herself to ask the question that she'd been dreading most of all. "Was I the only survivor?"

"Yes," her mother whispered. "I'm sorry, Lenora."

She was lying. Lenora pursed her lips. It wasn't that she'd expected her to confess to imprisoning everyone… but maybe some way to avoid the truth. Lenora met her gaze.

The lie had come easily, and her mother's wide blue eyes were glassy with fake empathy.

Her mother opened her arms, and Lenora allowed herself to be embraced. Instead of comforting, the closeness pricked every hair on Lenora's body. This woman was a monster.

Her mother stroked her hair. "It will be alright, Daughter. You're free now, and I have so much to teach you."

Free?

Did she think she was doing Lenora a favor? Despite learning of the captain's true intentions, a hollow ache burned in her chest. She sniffled, pushing away from her mother's arms.

"What do you mean you have so much teach me?"

"Your father's kept you away from the water your whole life, no doubt?"

Lenora nodded, afraid to speak. She felt defensive of Father's actions, even if she hadn't liked them.

"I suppose he discouraged you from singing?"

"Yes, he gets headaches easily, so he had me focus on cross-stitch rather than music."

"Rubbish. Lenora. He had you avoid the things that might show you were part siren."

"Oh."

"How're you feeling?"

She answered honestly, "Confused."

Her mother gave her a sympathetic smile and squeezed her shoulder. "No, I mean, are you physically well enough to go for a swim?"

"I-I think so."

"Follow me." Her mother smiled, revealing the sharp point of fangs.

Again, Lenora was reminded of the glimpse of the monster she'd seen on board, and she stifled a shudder. Was this beautiful young woman her mother's true form, or was the monster? She wasn't ready to ask.

Her mind raced as she padded behind her mother, down the hall that she'd emerged from with the tray of food. They passed two open doorways, one stocked with provisions and another appearing to be a bedroom. Lenora slowed as much as she dared, scanning the rooms in search of keys.

The hallway opened up ahead. The cavern grew wider, and the ground met the water.

Without explanation, her mother dove into it.

"Wait!" Lenora wore her gown from before the crash. It was stiff with dried salt water, but seemed the wrong thing for swimming; still, what other choice did she have?

Her mother had yet to resurface, and a bubbling wave of panic made Lenora's throat tighten. Her heart thrummed. Was she going to lose her mother again? Even if she was a monster, Lenora didn't want that.

The seconds ticked by, and Lenora remembered that sirens could breathe underwater. Was that what her mother was doing? And did that mean Lenora could? She'd never tried that she could remember. She hadn't been to the ocean since before her mother left.

Lenora dove. The cold emptied her mind for a moment before she blinked at her surroundings. Her eyes adjusted to the murky dark of the water. Her mother waved at her, pointing to her neck, as a torrent of bubbles floated past them. *Gills?*

Her mother fluttered her shimmering, opalescent, scaly tail around Lenora in a dizzying circle. Had her legs morphed into a tail when she hit the water? Or was there an additional step to make them appear? Lenora wished she'd been underwater to see the transformation. She flexed and unflexed her legs and toes, but nothing happened.

Lenora ran her hands along the smooth surface of her own neck. Her lungs burned with need for air, and she kicked toward the surface. Her mother yanked at her hand, filling her with a surging panic as her need for a breath increased.

Alarmed, Lenora pulled with all her might, but her mother shook her head, gripping her harder. Was her mother trying to drown her?

As darkness increased around the corners of her vision, she pulled in a gasping breath.

But it wasn't from her mouth.

Her hands flew to her neck again. Small slits had opened. Her mother mimed clapping, smiling. She pointed to Lenora's legs.

Unlike her mother, she didn't have a tail, but a series of shimmering scales dotted her skin. The sides sprouted feathery fins. When she kicked, it was easier to glide and turn.

Her mother pointed up, and they bobbed on the surface of the water.

Her mother laughed. "I wasn't sure what was going to happen!"

Lenora frowned.

"I wasn't going to let you drown. When I found you before, you were unconscious, but you also hit your head… that probably hindered your transformation."

Lenora kicked her legs. "Will I get a tail?"

"I don't think so… but you're the only half-siren I've ever met. I wasn't sure about your gills, but I suspected."

Her stomach twisted. "Can I grow large and transform?"

Her mother blinked her wide blue eyes. "Whatever for?"

"I'm curious if it's possible."

She must've read something on Lenora's face because she said, "We try to scare the hunters away with that form. It isn't who we are, not really. You won't know if you can do it until you feel threatened, and you'll need to be near the water, of course." She tugged at Lenora's sopping cap sleeve.

"We'll need to get you some more functional clothes, but let's go see your axolotl first."

"Loxi? He's alive?" Her heart raced.

"Of course! Oh dear, I'm sorry. I would've told you sooner… He's a sea creature. One of our own."

"But the salt water…"

"His tank and the fresh water kept him contained. I was so pleased when I saw him. I wasn't sure your father would keep him for you. Loxi isn't a normal salamander. Come, I'll show you."

Her mother dove again, and Lenora was forced to follow for the second time.

Chapter Eighteen
Loxi

Lenora struggled to keep up with her mother. Water tugged at the gills in her neck as she swam harder. What would happen if she opened her mouth to breathe? Would she choke on the water? Did the gills bring air to her lungs in a different way? Or was it all magic?

She'd dreamed of being a fairy as a child, discovering some secret affinity for magic that was rumored to exist in the other realms of Lurin.

But somehow being part siren didn't feel the same.

The murky water matched her dark thoughts. Her mother had said sirens scared sailors away, but Lenora had been on the receiving end, and it was much more vicious than a warning.

As far as being used as a token, like her mother suggested, Lenora wasn't sure that being a half-siren had the same efficacy as being a full-siren. Devonshire's ship had gone through numerous assaults while she was on board, although… the monsters had never managed to sink it.

Was this due to Lenora? At the time, she'd assumed it was the skill of the hunters that had saved their lives, taking out the creatures before they'd capsized the ship.

Creatures, like her mother.

Fighting to not get left behind, Lenora could barely see her mother's tail ahead of her. The woman seemed to have forgotten Lenora wasn't used to this kind of swimming.

She wasn't sure how much to push back. She needed to appear to be on her side.

Whatever Devonshire's intentions had been, she didn't approve of his or his crew's imprisonment.

And she wanted answers.

The water was clearer ahead. Coral lined the ocean floor in an array of color and beauty – more magnificent than anything she'd ever witnessed on land. Her heart squeezed, thinking of Devonshire's gift – the colorful new tank and coral he'd gotten for Loxi.

Had he only done these things because he wanted a siren on his ship? She didn't want to believe it.

"Loxi!" she shouted in the water, sending up a stream of bubbles.

The axolotl swam below her with several others. At her call, he jetted toward her, growing larger and larger. She hadn't realized how far away he'd been.

Her eyes widened, and her mother doubled over in silent laughter.

Loxi nudged her hand, and she petted his oversized snout. She swam around him, taking in his enlarged form – he was the size of a horse, whereas before he'd fit in her palm.

Another axolotl, a greenish-brown colored one, came over to her mother. She looped her arms around the axolotl's neck before staring pointedly at Lenora.

Lenora threw her leg over Loxi's back, leaning forward and holding around his neck like her mother had done with the other axolotl.

The axolotls took off, darting through the water in dizzying circles. It would've been impossible to retrace the path. Lenora's heart sped up, and she clung tighter to Loxi. They passed through vibrant schools of fish in vivid shades of sapphire and tangerine, as well as fields of verdant seaweed and dark rocky tunnels.

Off in the distance, she saw the floating remnants of a ship. Her eyes burned as she refused to blink. Was it her ship? It was impossible to tell, but it filled her with a sense of loss that she wouldn't have expected.

The water grew murkier, obscuring her view of the ocean's colors. Loxi swam closer to the surface, and her mouth gulped in a breath of the warm, dank cavern air. She didn't remember turning around, but they were back in her mother's home.

Her mother waited for her at the cavern's edge, squeezing water from her long black tresses. "Enjoy the ride?"

"Yes, it was beautiful."

She extended her hand toward Lenora, helping her from the water. "Axolotls and sirens have always been companions. They're our sworn protectors."

Lenora stared at Loxi, who bobbed in the water of the cavern. "I always felt like he could understand me, but sometimes I'd think I just imagined it."

Her mother rolled her eyes. "I'm sure your father put that idea in your head."

"No, no," Lenora insisted. "I never told him." Mention of Father brought up an opportunity for more questions. She licked the salt from her lips, considering what to ask. "What did he know about sirens? About you? About Loxi?"

Her mother sighed. "Let's get you out of that dripping dress first. Then I'll tell you everything."

Lenora's heart was in her throat as she followed her mother into the hall. She paused, staring down the distance of the cavern and thinking of her shipmates.

They went only a short distance, to the bedroom Lenora had assumed was her mother's. It held a wooden bed with a wide mattress and a fine wooden wardrobe. Lenora feigned interest, hoping to find a hidden spot for a key. "How did you get this furniture down here?"

Her mother rummaged inside the wardrobe, handing Lenora a dress similar to her own. "It's all from shipwrecks. It's taken me years to find something in decent shape."

The air went out of Lenora, imagining the people who died at sea for her mother to have some furniture.

Her mother walked past her. "I'll wait for you outside."

Lenora didn't waste the opportunity. She ripped her dress off and pulled on the new one in a flash, using the rest of the time to pat down the wardrobe and look under the pillows and mattress. Tears burned behind her eyes.

The key wasn't here.

"Ready?" her mother called from the hall.

Lenora yanked at the hem of her dress. The knotted garment was much shorter than she was used to and rough on her skin. Lenora longed for the soft, billowing fabric of her cotton dresses, but the seaweed dress would be much more practical for swimming. It was sleeveless, fitted, and cut just above her knees to freely kick, or in her mother's case, grow a tail.

Her mother balanced a round silver tray that held a tea service, and they went back to Lenora's room. The mismatched china rattled as her mother deposited the tray onto the rock slab Lenora had used for a bed before she pulled wooden stools from a corner. "I use this space for dining normally."

"Oh."

"You can keep it as your room or share mine. I wasn't sure which you'd prefer."

Lenora nodded, not answering.

"So you want to know about my relationship with your father." She passed Lenora a steaming teacup. It was white with painted flowers and a chipped rim. Her heart sank, thinking of whom it may have once belonged to.

Running her finger along the broken edge of her cup, she cleared her throat. "Yes."

Her mother misread the gesture. "Sorry, I have no cream or sugar. They never survive the crashes, I'm afraid."

Lenora met her eyes. "How did you meet Father?"

"On an island. I was curious about humans, and he was a sailor –"

Lenora nearly toppled her tea. "What?"

Her mother chuckled. "He never told you?"

Lenora shook her head.

"Well, he was a fine sailor. The best, in fact. At first, no one recognized me for what I was. I claimed to have survived a crash and have lost my memory. The island was full of life, teeming with resources and food, so the sailors lingered."

Lenora's fingers tightened on her cup.

"But then, of course, I couldn't stay out of the water. I went for a late-night swim, but some of the sailors saw me change. Your father protected me… I'd had weeks of opportunity to attack them, but I hadn't. The crew was split on what they should do with me."

Lenora's eyes widened.

Her mother looked away. "So I told them I could protect them from attack. I regretted this decision later, of course. I sealed my own fate. Your father saved me, but he also couldn't help himself from using me. He was handsome and brave. I fell for him the moment he had protected me, and I was unlike any of the refined, quiet women he was used to." She smiled for a moment as if enjoying the memory. "He loved me too, and for a while, I relished sailing and his affections. We married, and we were happy, but I missed the ocean and my freedom. After nearly a year at sea, your father brought me back to Oceanea." Her eyes grew glassy. "I hoped I would come to love it like I loved my island, but I was miserable. I couldn't risk someone seeing me swim. There were rumors, of course, spread by some of the sailors, but most people laughed them away. We had you, and it was a welcome distraction from my homesickness." She took a sip of tea. "But then I began to weaken. We didn't understand it at first and assumed it was some sort of illness, but it lasted for years. I'd take you to the ocean, hoping the brief contact would strengthen me, but it didn't help enough." She met Lenora's gaze. "I didn't want to leave you, Lenora. It was the last thing I wanted to do."

Lenora blinked back tears. "Father told me you died."

"I'm sorry. He couldn't tell people his wife had left him and be scandalized, and I'm sure he didn't want to risk having you come looking for me and lose you, too. Fortunately, you seemed strong and didn't seem to need the water – you loved it, of course, but your father became afraid that you'd grow to depend on it if you stayed in contact."

Lenora's heart sped up. That's why Father had kept her away from the ocean. Lenora didn't know what to say, so she fidgeted with her teacup. The dripping of the stalactites echoed in the silence. "Why do you think he had me get engaged to Captain Devonshire?"

Her mother chewed at her lip as if considering her words carefully. "We agreed that if you were allowed to grow up with him, he would return you to the sea by your eighteenth birthday." She put her cup down with a clatter. "But he promised you to that man. I think it was his way of fulfilling his promise to me while keeping you connected to his world."

Lenora remembered her father's ragged appearance and evident worry right before her engagement ceremony. Had he wanted her to stay? "I wish he had told me the truth. We could've come out here together to see you."

Her mother's mouth was a grim line. "No, Lenora. The sirens would have certainly killed him."

Lenora's heart pounded in her ears. "But you said –"

"We don't attack without provocation, but to our people, I was stolen. When I returned, I was so weak that no one thought I would survive. Your father really might have believed me to be dead." She forced a broken laugh.

"You could've visited."

Her mother quirked an eyebrow. "No, leaving once was painful enough, both emotionally and physically, and how was your father supposed to explain that? He couldn't have his dead wife showing up at his doorstep." She studied Lenora's face and hugged her again. "I'm sorry we put you through this. I've missed you so much."

Lenora swallowed, warming in her mother's embrace and wanting this moment to mean as much to her as it did to her mother.

If anything, it made her more depressed.

The story filled in missing pieces, but her mother still said nothing of her captives down the hall. If her parents had ended things so amicably, she didn't understand why her mother would trap the sailors. She wanted to believe her, but she suspected there were a great many things her mother had left out from their heart-to-heart.

Chapter Nineteen
Questions

"Lenora, we have to go," her mother whispered.

"Mmm." Lenora pushed herself up, rubbing the sleep from her eyes. She'd planned to sneak around the cavern once her mother had fallen asleep, but apparently she'd lost her chance.

"A ship has come into this area."

Lenora's heart sped up. "Can't you just let it sail by?"

Her mother huffed, blowing hair from her face. "No siren is safe. They'll come for us."

Lenora pulled her knees up to her chest.

"You don't believe me?" Her mother put her hands on her hips.

"When I was with Captain Devonshire, the sea creatures attacked us."

"After you invaded their home."

Lenora looked up from her knees. "But if they'd just let us sail by –"

"Is that what your captain told you?"

"It's what I saw."

Her mother paced. "I promise you, Lenora, Devonshire is known amongst our kind as a hunter."

Lenora bit at the inside of her cheek, trying to keep her features impassive. Was this the reason her mother had captured him?

She turned to her. "You never saw any sign of him seeking us out?"

Lenora's pulse pounded in her ears, thinking of the time in his cabin, assisting with the maps. She didn't want to give her mother more reasons to suspect the captain, so she said nothing.

"I want you to come with me, Lenora, so I can show you the truth."

"Fine. I'll come to observe, but I won't be attacking any ships."

Her mother smiled. "That's all I was hoping for… and to have you meet some of the others."

"Will we be safe?"

Her mother's gaze softened. "I'll keep you tucked away. You don't know how to use your voice yet, but you're welcome to try." She gestured ahead, and Lenora followed her to the water's edge. Her mother dove in, but Lenora hesitated.

Could she use this opportunity to search for the key?

Even though she wanted to save the crew, it felt devious, like she was betraying her mother's trust, even though the woman had imprisoned Lenora's friends.

Not friends, she corrected herself, *crew.* Who but Devonshire had paid her any mind? Indecision held her to the spot. Would her mother return and come looking for her?

Loxi's smiling face bobbed in the water.

Despite her worries, she smiled back, patting his broad, slippery snout. He huffed into her hand, showing his impatience at her indecision. She stood again, pacing the shore as she twisted a strand of hair around her finger. She wasn't sure if she wanted to witness an attacking ship or the other sirens, but obviously her mother had expected her to follow.

Her heart squeezed, thinking of the captive sailors again. She'd already wasted too much time, and truthfully, she did want to learn more about being a siren. Diving next to Loxi, Lenora wrapped her arms around his neck. She hoped her mother wouldn't notice her lagging. Without a thought, her fins appeared and her gills opened. She was glad it came quicker this time.

The axolotl zipped through the water, and Lenora squeezed her eyes shut.

Biting down on her lip, she tried to ignore her growing sense of dread. It was worse than waiting for Elisabeth and Thomas to arrive on the day of her party or getting engaged to a strange pirate. Those memories felt distant – like someone else's instead of mere weeks ago.

What would she see when she caught up to her mother? Dead sailors or dead sirens?

She'd decided to follow, but her muscles tensed as they drew nearer. Why did she want to learn about being a siren? She'd already seen firsthand their murderous, monstrous deeds.

Loxi bobbed into the open air.

The shock of cold had Lenora gasping. She sank back into the water, so only her eyes and top of her head surfaced. In the distance, she could see a large sailing vessel offshore of an island. Her heart clenched, and she clung to Loxi's neck. She didn't see her mother, nor any other sirens. Loxi swam them closer, as if reading her thoughts.

Yanking on his neck, she shouted under the water, "That's close enough!" and Loxi complied.

A shadowy figure stood on the shore.

Was that the siren?

What was she doing? Tingling with anticipation and worry, Lenora lifted her head out of the water. She spotted her mother just under the surface – only a few feet ahead of her and Loxi.

Lenora hugged Loxi tighter. Should she hide? They were a great distance away still, and she doubted anyone would look in her direction, but she held her breath.

A clamoring of men's voices rang out, but Lenora couldn't make out what they were saying.

The woman on the shore cried out, "Please leave!"

A spear flew at her, and Lenora gasped, but the siren had jumped out of the way into the water. More weapons were hurled after her, but she emerged unscathed and towering above their ship.

She no longer resembled the diminutive figure Lenora had seen, but a towering creature with a round, terrible mouth of jagged teeth, feathery blood-red wings, and wicked tentacles of hair, like the sirens that had attacked Lenora's ship. The creature sang:

"Weary sailors
Let us bring you rest
Stop your toiling
Believe what is best

Relax, visit
In the ocean deep
Never striving
Lying down to sleep."

The image of the monster flickered, replaced with a beautiful woman. Lenora felt drawn to her, and her mother grabbed at her hand, tugging her under the water. The ocean cleared her head. Was it her human side that made her susceptible to the siren's song? Unlike the men on her ship, she seemed to be able to fight it off somewhat; she hadn't dove into the water that first time they'd been attacked.

Covering her ears, she went to the surface again. As the siren flew above the ship, singing, the sailors' attacks slowed and then stopped. Men jumped overboard. The ship capsized. Lenora turned away and whispered to her axolotl. "Take me back, Loxi. I've seen enough."

Loxi complied, and her mother didn't stop her.

***

Lenora returned to the cavern, immediately bolting to the kitchen and storage pantry she hadn't searched yet. There was no hook for keys. She overturned cups, stacked bowls, and pots and pans, finding nothing. She looked through packages of food, canisters of loose tea, and the small waste bin before sinking to the floor.

The siren hadn't been the first to attack, nor had she attempted to hurt any of the sailors until after the first spear had been thrown, but the results of her song were the same. Drowned and dying men.

Had the creatures they encountered been defending themselves in the same way?

Lenora rubbed at her temples, trying to piece together every moment of her time at sea.

Devonshire had been hunting them. He had maps plotted. Her mother said some had gone on the offensive, but the lone woman she'd seen on the island hadn't been one of them.

Lenora should return to her room in case her mother returned or not be wasting time here, but memories of tracing and plotting maps with Devonshire squeezed her heart.

Was it possible that the sirens they had attacked would've left them alone? Had the crew gone on the offense like these sailors today? She couldn't remember each time clearly; usually, she'd been one of the last to grab her weapon.

She touched her earrings again, picturing the captain's smiling face. Whatever his reasons for making an agreement with Lenora's father, they were betrothed. She went back to the water, checking for a sign of her mother before darting through the rest of the cavern.

Whether her mother was a monster or a defender of her people, she was a liar, claiming Lenora was the only survivor of the crash while imprisoning the captain and crew.

Staring down the end of the hallway, Lenora's mind floated back to her ship with the unmarked door. If the captain had known about Lenora's mother, maybe he didn't want her to see the sirens in their human form for fear of recognizing them as her own kind?

The knowledge twisted in her gut.

How could she love a man who had kept that sort of secret?

Love.

The word had come to her unexpectedly. Did she love the captain? Something like affection and mutual respect had started between them, but she wasn't sure it had blossomed yet. Her heart pounded as she went to the end of the hallway. Perhaps her anger should outweigh her affections for Devonshire, but she was drawn to him nonetheless. She held her breath as she tried the knob again, but of course, it was locked.

Noise rose behind it.

She pressed her ear against the door. "How're you all fairing?"

"Lenora," her mother's voice made her jump. "What're you doing?"

"I-I..." Her face heated. She swallowed, trying to keep the quiver out of her voice and failing. "I thought I heard voices."

"Tell me what you saw today."

"What?" she squeaked, unnerved by the unexpected question.

Her mother crossed her arms.

"I saw a lone woman on an island attacked by a crew of people."

"Do you believe me now?"

Lenora nodded, without fully grasping her meaning.

"They hunt us, Lenora. That's why I did this." Without further explanation, she pulled a key from inside her dress and unlocked the door.

Chapter Twenty
The Prisoners

Her mother opened the door, revealing rows of cells. A murmur of excitement was replaced by a cacophony of angry shouts as Lenora's mother followed her inside.

"Captain!" Lenora ran over to Devonshire at once, reaching her hand through the bars of his cage. He pulled back, hesitant.

She dropped her arm, disappointment and confusion mingling together.

Devonshire's deep voice asked, "Lenora, are you working with the sirens?"

The crew hushed, watching with interest.

"She's my mother." Her voice caught, but he didn't flinch or look surprised. "You knew?"

Her mother walked over, scowling. "Tell her, Captain."

Devonshire squeezed the bridge of his nose. "This woman is a monster. You can't trust anything she says."

Lenora recognized the change of subject for what it was. "What about you, Captain?" she whispered. "What secrets have you been keeping?" Her heart clenched, and her stomach twisted in knots. After days apart, she had wanted a warm greeting, some sign of his affection, but he was the one in a cage. What had Lenora expected him to do?

He met her eyes then. "Yes, Lenora, I knew you were part siren, but I didn't know she was your mother or that you'd be willing to work with them."

"I-I'm not."

Her mother frowned. "Tell her all of it, human."

His eyes darted between them. "I wanted to marry you because you were part siren. I had hoped you would keep my ship safe from attack."

She pulled away from him, like she'd been burned with hot water. Did he still feel nothing for her? She scanned the men's faces, but no one looked surprised. She whispered, "Everyone… knew?"

Devonshire nodded. The crew's distant behaviors made more sense now. She'd assumed it was because she was a woman, but if they'd known she was part siren…

"Her father told you?" Her mother crossed her arms.

"Yes, but I promised to protect her… from you." He spat.

"What? Why from her?" Lenora clutched at the bars.

"Lenora, you have to trust me. I kept away from you at first, thinking I shouldn't let myself grow affectionate, but I did anyway. I –"

"Enough!" her mother snapped. "You used my daughter to kill her own people, her own family, and protect your own cowardly hide."

His eyes widened. "Lenora, ask her about the rest of the crew –"

Lenora counted maybe fifty men crowded in several cages. How many were missing?

"They drowned," Her mother interjected.

"At your hand!" Devonshire yelled.

"It was the storm. You should be grateful I was able to save so many of you and your fiancée."

Lenora allowed her mother to pull her back into the hallway. Devonshire's brown eyes silently pleaded with her until they were outside the room.

Her mother exhaled, keeping her voice low. "Truthfully, I don't know what to do with them, Lenora. I want to be rid of them, but now that Devonshire has found our nest, I don't trust him and his men not to kill us."

"I can make him promise."

She lifted her dark, thin eyebrows. "Lenora, have you heard nothing? It was a marriage of convenience for him. Nothing more. I will not risk my safety, our people's, or yours."

"I could never hurt them."

"You won't have to."

"Please, don't kill them. I've grown to care for the captain…"

Her mother groaned, not meeting Lenora's eyes. "Fine. I will let them go. We'll have the axolotls bring them to the nearest ship or island."

Chin quivering, Lenora embraced her mother, thankful she meant it this time.

***

Devonshire glared daggers at her mother as she unlocked the crewmen, releasing groups of four at a time. Two men could ride each axolotl. They rushed away, not even bothering to glance in Lenora's direction. She sat on the cavern floor, watching the tense truce. It was painstakingly slow, having to wait for the axolotls to return.

But Lenora had to see for herself, to ensure it was really happening. Devonshire was released last, and she was thankful for the extra time with him, even if she didn't know what he was feeling.

Her mother frowned at him, hesitating before pulling open the barred door. "Your crew held up their end of the bargain. One wrong move, and you'll hear my song."

Devonshire nodded, stepping toward Lenora. He swept her up into his arms, kissing her cheek and setting her face on fire.

"Let's go."

He wants me to come with him.

The words sent shivers of excitement through her, but she hesitated. "I'm going to stay."

"What?"

"Promise you'll not come looking for me or the sirens again."

"I cannot do that."

Lenora stiffened at the declaration. Her mother snorted.

"I convinced my mother you were a man of honor that could be trusted. Please don't prove me wrong. Make your crew promise as well when you're back with them."

"What kind of man would leave his fiancée in the company of monsters?"

Lenora stepped closer to the captain. "A wise man who recognizes a good deal when it's offered to him."

His throat bobbed. "Lenora... on the ship earlier... Did you hear?"

She shook her head. "No."

"I'm sorry for wasting our time together pretending I didn't care for you... I was scared and foolish."

Even though her mother was watching, and Lenora trembled, she grabbed Devonshire's face into her hands, kissing him before she could lose her courage. He flinched before relaxing and wrapping his arms around her waist, deepening the kiss.

Lenora's whole body hummed, but he pulled away only seconds later.

"I don't want to leave you."

She shook her head. "I have to stay. There's this whole part of my life I've only just started learning about."

Devonshire squeezed her hand. "We will see each other again." His deep brown eyes held hers, and then he was gone, being pulled into the hallway by her mother. She trailed behind them, watching him take a deep breath as Loxi plunged himself into the water.

"How far is the surface?" Lenora asked, furrowing her brow.

Her mother sighed. "He'll be fine. Loxi is an incredibly fast swimmer."

Lenora hesitated, resisting the desire to chase after him. Saying goodbye a second time wouldn't make it any easier.

"I'm glad you decided to stay," her mother whispered, wiping at Lenora's tears.

Lenora sniffled. "Thank you for letting them return. I couldn't bear the idea of anything ever happening to the captain or his men because of me."

Her mother extended her hand, and Lenora took it. She led Lenora to her stony bed, pulling a blanket to her shoulders.

Lenora closed her eyes, and her mother stroked her hair, humming a melody she remembered from her youth.

***

Lenora woke later, unsure of how much time had passed.

Her mother stood in the doorway, damp from a swim. "Oh, good, you're up. I wanted to let you get your rest, but there's a ball tonight at one of the nobility's homes. They're old friends of mine, and I thought it'd be fun for you to get to meet more of our people."

"A ball?"

"Yes, we can't let humans have all the fun." She winked. "It's the season. I don't suppose you're interested in the marriage market..."

Lenora gasped. "Mother, I'm already engaged."

"To a human. That hardly counts."

Lenora's hand went to her earrings. "It does to me."

Her mother patted her shoulder. "I have the perfect dress for you."

They went to her bedroom, where she rummaged through her wardrobe, pulling out a gown that made Lenora gasp. She would've thought it'd be impossible to make an opulent gown of seaweed and sea shells, and she would've been wrong.

Her mother helped her to slip it on.

The seaweed was covered in the shiny, pale pink and white shells. She spun, watching the tightly woven fabric sparkle as the intricate beading of hundreds of shells caught the light. Her mother clapped her hands together. "You look gorgeous!"

"Thank you," she smiled, running her hands along the skirts. "It may be the most beautiful gown I've ever worn."

Her mother sighed. "It'll be a pain to swim in, weighted down by all the shells, but Loxi will do the hard part." She winked. Her mother wore a simpler gown with longer sleeves and a zigzagging pattern of glowing thread along the hemline of the same material as her canopied hallway.

They waited for several minutes for Loxi, but he still hadn't returned.

Lenora's stomach twisted. "Do you think they've had some sort of trouble?"

"No, my dear, I'm sure he's resting after all the swimming back and forth from the surface. Ride my axolotl with me. Pearl won't mind."

The brownish-green axolotl shook her head along the surface of the water, indicating that she did mind, but her mother was already in the water, so Lenora followed.

With two gowned passengers, they moved much slower than before. Lenora preferred it. She could keep her eyes open, studying details of her underwater home she hadn't been able to notice before.

Along the brightly colored coral, there was a cleared path. Occasionally, there were branches running in different directions, which the axolotl followed. Lenora could see remains of ships, bits of wood, cracked tea sets, frayed rope, and rusted pieces of unrecognizable metal. Each bit of evidence saddened her, reminding her that the sirens were likely responsible for the crashes.

Other axolotls swam in the distance, with passengers who waved.

Pearl ducked inside a cave, plunging them into darkness. Lenora clung to her mother until they emerged into the light and bobbed to the surface.

Sandy shore and waves crashed at the base of a large estate, whose stairs extended into the ocean. Lenora had been expecting a cavern, much like her mother's, instead of a home like Father's.

Her mother swam to the shore, calling back to Pearl. "We'll be back when the moon is at its height!"

Lenora still clung to the axolotl. Pearl bucked her off, splashing her back into the water.

Chapter Twenty-One
The Party

Lenora ran through the surf, catching up to her mother.
"When you said ball –"

"You pictured an underwater cavern like my own? Like I told you earlier, Lenora, we used to all live on the islands before we were driven underwater or up on unreachable cliffs. This home has remained because of the miles of rocky caverns in the shallow waters around it. No boat can even come close." She gave a sad smile.

Dozens of others emerged from the water, but a few flew through the darkness of the night sky, landing on the sand with grace before pulling their wings back into their bodies. Like her mother, they all had black hair and nearly translucent skin, but their features were as different as the people of Oceanea's.

"Can this be your daughter, Circe?"

Lenora curtseyed.

The woman who spoke still donned her wings. Up close, Lenora could see how beautiful they were – gold flecks mixed with an array of crimson. From a distance, the wings had always seemed an ominous symbol – the blood-red warning of an imminent death. Her eyes widened at Lenora's perusal.

"Have you not seen wings before?"

"Not this close. They're stunning."

The woman trilled a laugh.

Her mother guided her inside, and Lenora wondered if she'd done something wrong. The sea glass foyer shimmered from hundreds of flaming candles. Canopies, much like the ones in her mother's cavern, lined the ceiling, sparkling like starlight.

Shells were used throughout the noble's mansion, but other than that, the styles of furniture and decor reminded her much of the finer homes on Oceanea. A wave of homesickness squeezed her heart. As much as she wanted to understand this part of herself, she missed her father and her old life.

She stepped into the ballroom, expecting much of the same, but the ceiling and walls opened to the night sky. The room was a floor with pillars draped with glowing lights and nothing else. Tables lined the inner wall of the house, stuffed with every kind of seafood delicacy imaginable. Lenora's stomach grumbled.

Her mother offered her a plate. Lenora had been up most of the night, watching the crew's departure, and had slept the day away without eating. Stuffing the small plate, she sampled everything. A chorus sang a lively melody, arranging their voices much like instruments.

A young handsome man walked toward Lenora as she took another large bite of something salty and pungent. *Ugh.* She tried to swallow it but found she could not. Coughing, she spat the offensive morsel into a napkin.

Her mother rolled her eyes, and Lenora's face heated.

The stranger chuckled, studying her. He was tall with jet black hair, the same ocean blue eyes, and pale, clean-shaven skin. He'd seen her unladylike reaction, but his wide smile put her at ease as he bowed to Lenora. "May I have this dance, my lady?"

Her mother smiled and nodded. "Go on. Have fun."

Lenora allowed herself to be guided to the dance floor. Nerves kicked in as they turned and stepped around each other. Mimicking the movements around her, Lenora enjoyed being passed along the dance floor from partner to partner.

But she missed Devonshire.

This strange new life felt like the one she'd been destined for, so why did she miss her distant fiancé?

Scanning the crowd of happy faces, she decided her mother must've stepped away from the dance. Lenora searched the table of refreshments but didn't see any drinks. She went back into the emptied foyer and wandered down a hall, hunting for a server or the kitchen.

"Hi," a deep voice startled her.

She shrieked.

The handsome stranger she'd danced with held out his hand. "Sorry, I didn't mean to startle you. I'm Cetus, by the way. Are you looking for something?"

"Punch."

He guided her back in the direction she'd come. "The bowl must've just been emptied when you came looking. It should be refilled by now. Our servants have been running laps back and forth to the kitchen all night."

"Oh." She realized he must live in this house, meaning he was either the nobleman or his son – it was hard to tell when sirens didn't age like humans. Was it rude of her to be roaming the hallways unescorted? He'd already seen her spit out some of his food. She didn't want to offend him. Fidgeting with a shell on her dress, she searched for polite conversation.

He broke the silence. "Are you enjoying your time here amongst your own people?"

"You know who I am?" Her eyebrows shot up.

"Of course, our mothers are old friends, but I doubt anyone here doesn't already know all about you, Lenora. There are rumors of other half-sirens, descendants of our people that have settled in the far corners of Lurin, but I haven't met one before tonight."

Her face flushed. "So it's not just my imagination that people are staring at me?"

He laughed. "No, that isn't entirely unfounded, I'm afraid. Come, let me grab you some punch, and maybe another dance?"

Lenora smiled and curtseyed. "I'd be delighted."

***

Hours later, Lenora's mother found her. "You seem like you had a good time tonight."

"I did," she admitted. "Though I would've liked to spend more time together. Where did you go?"

Her mother evaded the question. "I saw you and Cetus getting on."

"Yes, he's a wonderful dance partner."

"He's your betrothed."

"Wh-what?"

"Well…" her mother guided her from the manor, back onto the sand. "His parents and I reached an understanding years ago. Obviously, I didn't know your father planned to promise you to another human before returning you home."

Lenora's heart sped up. "But surely you explained…"

"Lenora, do you intend to leave?"

"I don't know what –"

"Unless you plan on returning to Oceanea, it doesn't matter who you were previously engaged to, and I hardly think a forced ceremony with a pirate using you for your gifts counts as a valid arrangement."

Lenora's face heated. Her engagement had been forced upon her, but she had grown to care for the captain.

She wasn't sure what she wanted.

He had kept secrets from her, but she had to believe he had come to care for her the way she had for him. He had seemed to be saying as much earlier when her mother had interrupted him. She'd wished she'd heard all of it, or had probed him about what he'd said during the crash, but at least she had gotten up the nerve to kiss him.

Still, her mother was right. If she stayed here, she would no longer be promised to Captain Devonshire. She blinked back tears, staring out at the lapping, moonlit waves of the ocean.

What would the Maker have her do? He'd made her half-siren and reunited her with her long-lost mother… but she hadn't considered if this was the path she was meant to follow.

Her mother squeezed her hand. "Just think about it, Lenora. I won't force you to do anything. That's the human way, not the siren's."

Chapter Twenty-Two
Singing

Loxi still hadn't returned, and Lenora felt guilty about her carefree evening. Her mother waved off her concerns as she pulled off her heavy dress.

"It's probably nothing," she assured Lenora. But her brow furrowed, confessing her true thoughts. She hurried away, and Lenora listened from the hallway as she instructed Pearl.

"Find Loxi," she snapped. "Ask the others to help you and don't return until you do."

Lenora was surprised by her short-tempered command and slipped back into her bedroom before her mother could notice her eavesdropping.

Her mother had brought in the pink silken pillow, placing it next to her own. Lenora laid down, relishing the softness of a real mattress after days of sleeping on a hard rock. She intended to stay awake and ask more questions, but she drifted off before her mother returned.

***

The next morning, Lenora stretched, running her hand along the cold spot next to her on the bed. Had her mother slept? She threw her feet over the side as her mother arrived with the breakfast tray, with two steaming cups of tea and biscuits.

Her mother smiled, beaming with radiance. She certainly looked like she'd slept. "These were found in a sealed metal tin. They're still fresh."

"Thank you." Lenora grabbed at one of the cookies before taking a tentative sip of the scalding tea. "I didn't hear you get up."

"Yes, you were exhausted."

"Is Loxi back?"

Her mother's smile fell. "No, I'm afraid not. Pearl has gone looking, so there's nothing to worry about."

"We need to go looking for him."

Her mother patted her knee, masking her previous concern. "No, he'll come to us, dear. We can't exactly search the ocean." Lenora thought to protest, but her mother cut her off. "Let's work on singing today and sprouting your wings."

Lenora dropped her breakfast. "You think I'll be able to? Have wings, I mean?" Lenora wasn't sure she wanted to learn any siren songs. The only one she was familiar with led to men drowning.

"Of course you'll be able to have wings! You've grown gills and a few fins. Singing, I expect, will come the most naturally of all of it." Her mother held a note. "See if you can match mine."

Lenora tried, but her mother frowned.

"Let's try warming up your voice first."

She made a series of ridiculous trilling noises, and Lenora tried to mimic them.

She hummed, and Lenora matched her note.

"That was much better this time. Now, the trick with your wings is much like growing your fins or opening your gills; it comes when you need it to. Imagine you want to fly over a vast valley."

Her mother hummed, demonstrating. Her wings grew from her back in rapid succession, feather after feather in mere seconds.

"Does it hurt?" Lenora asked, examining her back.

"Not at all, though it'll take you more effort and be much slower at first."

Lenora nodded and hummed, but nothing happened.

"Try closing your eyes," her mother encouraged.

Lenora tried again.

"Are you picturing the valley?"

"Yes." Lenora dropped her shoulders. Maybe she wasn't meant to have wings.

"Picture a more urgent situation, like falling to your death."

Lenora's eyes flew open.

"I know that sounds horrible, but remember what happened with your gills. They didn't open till you really needed a breath."

Lenora closed her eyes again. She let her heart speed up, thinking of falling through the air, and she hummed. Her back tingled, and her eyes shot open once more. "Did anything happen?"

Her mother smiled. "I think I saw the start of a feather. You have to wait longer, really hold the note." She patted the area above her stomach. "You need to feel the note deep inside your body. You'll know you have it when the wings open. It's a bit like stretching in the morning after a long night's sleep."

Lenora squeezed her eyes shut, pushing herself and singing until her body hummed with magic and her wings extended. She turned, examining the feathers, both delighted and overwhelmed. They looked identical and as wide and capable of flight as any other siren's, but were deep blue in color. What would it be like to fly with them?

Her mother clapped her hands together. "I knew you could do it!"

***

Lenora practiced several more times before they went back to the water's edge to check on the axolotls. Loxi still hadn't returned, and neither had Pearl. Lenora had never been without her salamander, and she started to imagine the worst when she saw a snout emerge from the water.

"Loxi!" she started, but as the pale creature emerged, she could tell it wasn't her pet, and it was being ridden by Cetus.

"Lenora," he greeted. "I was wondering if you'd like to join a group of us –"

"I made my wings appear!" she interrupted, before clapping a hand over her mouth.

His eyes widened. "That's amazing, Lenora! Are you busy now?"

"No, I don't think so." She turned to see the smiling figure of her mother leaning in the cavern's doorway.

"She's not," her mother said. "Have a good time, you two."

It wasn't until Lenora was zipping through the water with Cetus that it occurred to her about the impropriety of the situation. She was alone with a strange man. It seemed the manners and societal rules of sirens differed from Oceanea's, but it was hard to undo years of training after only days in this strange new world.

She wanted to ask him who was going to be at this get-together and what they were doing, but she knew he wouldn't be able to hear her until they emerged above water.

Cetus's axolotl bobbed on the surface. A few sirens splashed in the water, and several more were on the shore. Lenora recognized a couple faces from the party.

Her stomach clenched. Why had she agreed to come? What did she have in common with a group of siren teenagers? She squeezed water from her long, dark tresses, eager to have something to do with her hands.

Cetus led her gently by her elbow. "Let me introduce you to everyone."

Chapter Twenty-Three
The Cliff

Cetus showed up the next day and the next. Lenora enjoyed her life with her new freedoms. She could come and go as she wanted. She was learning to use magic, getting better at swimming and flying, and most amazing of all, the other sirens seemed to enjoy her company.

Cetus waved goodbye as another one of their friends left. She stared after their friend and his axolotl, thinking of Loxi.

Loxi had been missing for days, and as well as things were going, it left a hollow ache in her chest. Lenora kicked at some sand, dipping her chin to hide the flow of tears that had started down her face.

Cetus put his arm around her. "Thinking of Loxi again?"

She sniffed. "Yeah."

She met his eyes. Her face heated as she realized it was just the two of them.

"Join me for a picnic today. My favorite spot on this island is on the cliffs. You haven't seen them yet, right?"

She shook her head. "Only from here."

He smiled. "Come on."

They walked along the shore until they were feet from where the towering cliffside met the ocean. It was hundreds of feet up, nearly perpendicular, rocky and unscalable, like the side of a giant mountain was cut in half.

Lenora craned her neck as Cetus led her closer. "We're going up there?" she asked with a squeak.

Cetus laughed. "I should be able to carry you if you don't feel comfortable flying."

"No, I-I want to try."

She closed her eyes, picturing her wings unfurling, and sang, deep from her gut as her mother instructed her. Cetus's voice joined hers, harmonizing.

Her wings flickered and formed along her back, much like the uncurling of her fingers from a clenched fist. It was easier to do with her heightened nerves.

"That's the quickest they've appeared!"

Cetus winked, and she flushed. "You look even more beautiful with them."

Her face reddened at the compliment. "Do we need to return to your house? For the food?"

He smiled sheepishly, rubbing at his neck. "I actually set it all up before I came to get you. I was optimistic you'd say yes."

Her face heated further, and she was thankful when he took off into the air. She flapped behind him, turning and swaying off course with any sudden gust of wind. When she landed, her legs trembled.

Two golden goblets filled with juice, lobsters, and heaping skewers of fruit were laid out on a blanket, only a few feet from the rocky edge.

She gasped. "This must've taken you hours!"

"Well, I had the help of my servants, so don't give me too much credit."

Lenora sighed, touching her loose, wind-blown tresses. "I've already forgotten what it's like to have a lady's maid." She also wished she was wearing a gown for such a lovely date, instead of her short, simple seaweed frock. Folding her legs underneath herself, she tried to sit as ladylike as possible.

Cetus smiled, handing her a goblet of juice before sitting beside her. He leaned close, whispering into her ear. "Well, you'll have to get used to it again, once we're married."

Her mouth hung open, shocked by his boldness.

Laughing, he said, "Relax, Lenora, I'm hoping to get to know you better before we finalize our plans."

"About that…" she fiddled with one of her ears.

"I know about your *'engagement,'*" he said the word sarcastically. "But we were already promised to each other before all that, so it hardly counts. You should take those earrings out."

Lenora blinked, not meeting Cetus's deep blue eyes, and thinking of Devonshire. She tried to stay angry at the captain for using her and his deceit, but when she thought of the last time they saw each other… of his pleading brown eyes and their brief kiss, electricity zipped up her spine, setting her whole body on fire. She cleared her throat. "I think it counts."

Cetus gathered up her hands. "It's your choice, Lenora, but I hope you choose me, and not just because I don't trust the humans."

Lenora started on her lobster with the small fork provided. Cetus stared at her, ignoring the food.

"Aren't you going to eat?" she asked.

He shrugged.

She shrank under the intensity of his gaze and searched her mind for polite conversation. "What else do you like to do besides cliffside picnics and spending time with friends?"

"I enjoy dancing and flying, but I also take my duties seriously."

"Duties?"

"My family leads the sirens against the human threat. We strategize to keep them away. We're looking for more islands like this one to keep us safe."

"I-I didn't know. What does it feel like to be friends with one?"

"We're more than friends, Lenora, and you're only part human. I can tell you aren't like them."

She swallowed another bite of food with difficulty. "Th-thank you."

"Your mother cautioned me on talking to you about them, but I can tell you're on our side."

Avoiding an answer, she shoveled in a large piece of lobster meat she'd managed to extract from the tail. She practically choked on the overly big bite, and Cetus refilled her glass with a smile.

"Your mother says you don't need them to survive."

"Mmm, " she mumbled while chewing, trying not to reveal her utter confusion.

"If we could, I'd hunt those beasts to extinction, but then we'd age just like them."

Lenora went hot and cold all over and choked.

Cetus gently patted her back.

She coughed, taking another deep sip of her drink. "Have you forgotten I was raised among them? I am part human, too." Her heart sped up as the wind rustled her long, dark hair. She had thought Cetus was her friend, and that he was charming, but she no longer felt safe with him. In fact, his charm felt eerily similar to the siren song, full of promise that leads to death.

He tsked. "I guess I should've heeded your mother's warning."

"Yes, you should have," she said pointedly, squaring her shoulders. "What did you mean before about hunting them to not age like them?"

He laughed, and Lenora resisted the impulse to throw her drink in his face. "You really know nothing, do you? Well, you'd find out soon enough. Our siren song pulls out its victims' lives. It feeds us, extending our own life and youth. If I hadn't intercepted you at the party, then you would've seen for yourself. The partygoers were enjoying a feast of your crewmen in the back dining room of my family's manor."

She stood, trembling, beginning to sing. Her wings uncurled – she didn't have to imagine her terror this time.

Cetus grabbed her roughly, throwing a hand over her mouth, and her feathers flashed away. "You have to promise not to tell your mother. She'd kill me if she found out I told you."

"You think you deserve a favor from me! You're a murderer! Let me leave at once, if you have any honor."

He stepped back, lifting his hands as if becoming aware of how forceful he was being. "Of course. I only wanted a chance to explain things better. Sirens deserve to be able to feed on them, Lenora. They are without purpose, without magic. The Maker has made them weak. They are meant to be our prey."

She gasped, clutching at her chest. Did her mother feel the same? Cetus's words, *We'd age just like them,* echoed in her mind. Her stomach revolted, threatening to return the lobster she'd managed to eat.

Mother's perfect lineless smile flashed in her mind – she looked different from the mothers of Oceanea, closer to Lenora's age than a woman in her 40s or 50s. Lenora assumed it was a siren trait, but now… now…

"What about Mother?" she asked in a hushed tone.

Cetus smirked; a glint of cruelty flashed in his eyes. "She's the most bloodthirsty woman I've ever known."

"No, I don't believe you."

"Ask her what happened to that crew of yours. Better yet, ask her about that fiancé of yours. Ask her…"

Lenora stepped away from Cetus, not hearing him anymore as her pulse rushed in her ears, drowning out his words and the crashing waves in the distance below. She opened her mouth, singing, singing for all she was worth, but instead of sprouting wings, she grew, her limbs extending within seconds. She towered over the cliff side picnic.

He cackled. "What're you going to do with me, Lenora? Eat me, like we eat them?"

She attempted to answer, but her mouth had changed, round and full of razor-sharp teeth. Her tongue lashed against the roof of her mouth, but instead of words, she roared. Turning quickly, she threw herself into the ocean.

She hadn't even considered how dangerous a decision like that was until she fell through the air – she only knew she needed to get away from that siren boy. Something primal and insatiable rose inside of her.

She didn't trust herself not to kill him.

She thought she might sprout her wings, but she plummeted helplessly. A horrible splash jetted into the air as she sank into the cool ocean water. The water helped her come back to herself. Her form shrank back to her regular size, and her heart slowed. She kicked her finned legs, beginning the long swim back to her mother's cavern – she rode on the back of Cetus's axolotl when he had picked her up. Tears pricked her eyes, melding seamlessly in the current of ocean water.

She wasn't sure how to feel about being able to transform into the monstrous form of a siren – on the one hand, she'd no longer felt threatened by Cetus, but on the other, she resembled the monsters she hated. The ones who attacked the innocent people of Oceanea.

As she thought of everything she wanted to say to her mother, she was thankful for the winding distance between the two estates. Several times, the shadows of large fish gave her pause, causing her to worry Cetus had followed her.

If her mother fed on humans, had she done the same with Devonshire or the remaining crew that she'd imprisoned? What did Cetus mean 'ask her about that crew of yours' and 'that fiancé'?

He'd already implied they fed on them at the party. Had she lied about most of the crew drowning? Perhaps her mother hadn't freed Devonshire or the remaining men? Perhaps she…

No, it was too horrible a thought.

Lenora tried to push away her growing sense of dread. But what else could Cetus have meant than her mother had killed them? Kicking harder, Lenora swam on, pushing her body physically to repress the helplessness of her situation. If Devonshire and the crew were already dead, what could she do?

Her head pounded as well as her heart. If Cetus was being truthful, she'd confront her mother and leave this awful place.

But it didn't feel like enough.

She wasn't anyone's hero. She was a weak woman from Oceanea who had been lied to over and over again.

First by her father. Then by Devonshire. And finally, her mother.

Maker help her. She was a trusting fool.

Lenora's mind whirled. She'd dropped her head, swimming with all her might, and collided with an axolotl.

Chapter Twenty-Four
The Monster

Pearl frowned, swimming circles around her.

"Don't try to stop me, Pearl!" Lenora shouted in the water with a stream of bubbles.

The axolotl rolled her eyes, pointing to her back with her tail.

Should she trust her? The axolotl was loyal to her mother, but she knew nothing of what had transpired… hopefully. Lenora always had the sense that Loxi could read her mind, and she hadn't been around Pearl or other axolotls enough to know if it was a creature trait or their own unique bond.

Lenora pointed and unpointed her toes, trying to relieve the cramping that had started in her calves. Pearl smirked, watching her.

Sighing, Lenora threw a leg over Pearl's back before the axolotl darted through the water. She took a sharp right, past the ship wreck Lenora had come to think of as a marker for the cavern – that meant they weren't going to her mother's home.

She tightened her grip around the axolotl's neck as they slowed behind a large arching piece of the hull. A pale pink head popped into view.

"Loxi!"

Her axolotl wagged his tail in greeting. His delicate skin was patterned with slashes.

She petted his smooth, wide snout before leaning her head against his, *What happened to you?* she thought.

He pointed with his tail, back in the direction of the cavern.

Mother?

He nodded.

Pearl swam off to the side. She'd brought Lenora here. *Was she helping Loxi?*

Loxi nodded again.

Devonshire… her heart squeezed at the thought.

Loxi pointed up with his tail.

Did that mean… *he's alright?*

Loxi nodded. She hugged him, giving a warbled, choked sob. Crying felt more stilted under the water, like trying to run in mud, slower and less satisfying, but her heart soared in relief. Devonshire was alive.

The pair of axolotls awaited her instructions. Should she flee to Oceanea? Look for Devonshire? Or confront her mother?

She knew what the right thing to do was, but it wasn't the one she wanted to choose. Hugging Loxi one last time, she jumped onto Pearl's back.

***

When she bobbed to the surface of the stony cavern, Lenora still hadn't settled on what to say. She pushed out of the water, squeezed her long dripping hair, and paced the rocky floor.

Her mother leaned her head inside the doorway. "I thought I heard you in here. I hadn't expected you back so soon."

Lenora's whole body trembled. Her mind erased her practiced speeches and recalled only accusations. She eats them!

"What is it, Sweetheart?" her mother asked gently. The empathy in her words only grated Lenora further.

Lenora's heart raced."Y-you've been lying to me."

"Pardon?" Her mother's eyes widened.

Without thinking, Lenora snapped, "You eat them!" She took a deep breath in and out. "You kill humans to extend your own life."

Her mother's mouth straightened into a thin line. "Cetus told you." It wasn't a question, so Lenora said nothing. "I knew I couldn't trust him, but the way you two looked at each other... who am I to stand in the way of true love?"

Lenora scoffed. "True love? He's a monster. You're all monsters as far as I'm concerned. How could you do such a thing? You were married to a human. You have a human daughter."

"I'm not like Cetus. I don't hate them, Lenora, but I don't want to die either, so when a mass of bloodthirsty hunters crashes into my waters... Well, what would you do?"

"Is that really a question? I wouldn't kill them."

"Even at the cost of your own life?"

"You're twisting my words. You weren't defending yourself when you fed off drowning sailors."

"Drowning, exactly. They would've died anyway... And I saved some of them and your captain."

"To feed off of later?" Lenora asked shrilly.

Her mother huffed, narrowing her eyes. "I thought Devonshire could prove useful, which he did. I wanted to know how far the humans had gotten in tracking us. He refused to tell me anything, but when I realized he was your betrothed and your father had played me, well... It's for the best you found out before you married him."

"Did you return him?"

Her mother's eyelid twitched.

"Tell me."

"I was worried they'd come back, harm us, or take you; he implied as much when you said your goodbyes."

"That doesn't give you the right –"

"Doesn't it?" She took a step forward, narrowing her eyes. "Your axolotl attacked me when I tried to take him. They're linked to us by our thoughts and wishes. That shows where your loyalties lie. Would you really choose that man your father forced on you over your own mother?"

Lenora's heart sped up as she took a step back. "I was raised as a human. Can't you understand why I'm against this? I'm not choosing him. I'm –"

A hand grabbed her from behind. She screamed. Cetus twisted her arm behind her back. "We can't let her return home. She's seen too much."

Her mother sighed, squeezing at the bridge of her nose. "I know, I know."

Cetus grabbed hold of Lenora's head, squeezing both sides firmly. At first, she didn't realize what he planned to do. He didn't move. He just held her there tightly. Her mother's eyes widened.

"Stop!" Her mother threw her hand out. "Don't kill her. It would be a waste. Put her in one of the cages in the back. We can feed on her."

"But she's part siren…"

"She's part human, too. It should work."

Lenora trembled as Cetus lessened his grip. She should run… she should… He twisted her arm behind her back again, forcing her down the hall. Her mother led the way, unlocking the room and stepping aside.

She wouldn't meet Lenora's eyes as Cetus slammed the metal cage shut, the same one that had held Devonshire.

Chapter Twenty-Five
Escape

The minutes ticked by, and Lenora gave up the hope that her mother would return for her. She rattled her cage, already knowing if there was a way to break out of it by force, Devonshire would've done it. Dropping to the floor, she ran her hands along her arms, trying to escape the sudden chill.

"We can feed on her."

Her mother's words echoed back to her again and again. She curled onto her side, submitting to her exhaustion. Closing her eyes, she tried to let the warm embrace of sleep overtake her, but her mind betrayed her.

"We can feed on her. We can feed on her."

Father would never know what had happened to her. She thought of her anger toward him with regret. He had lied to her, but she still loved him. The words of his letter came back to her.

No doubt you are confused with my decision, but please know that I love you. I send you into Captain Devonshire's capable hands, believing he can keep you safe where I cannot, and grant you the freedom you no doubt long for.

Had he thought the captain could protect her from her own mother? He must've thought there was reason for concern if he'd married her off to someone who hunted sirens.

Hot tears rolled down her cheeks. The worry and sorrow she'd seen on her father's face the day of the ball had been real.

She sobbed, drifting off into fitful sleep laced with nightmares of the crash, siren attacks, and her mother.

A click of the door woke her.

Her mother rushed to the cage, unlocking it. "You have to get out of here, now."

"But…"

"I know what I said. The others will kill me if they find out. I'll come up with a story they'll believe. You have to leave. It's the only way to protect you…"

"Mother," she sobbed.

Her mother hugged her before pushing her away. "Go now. Cetus returned home, but he plans to come back with others."

Loxi bobbed in the water, awaiting her return. She dove next to him, letting him guide her through the water. Her heart pounded until they'd been riding for what felt like an hour. She began to relax, to believe she'd make it home. Thoughts of seeing Oceanea, Devonshire, and Father crowded away concerns over danger until Loxi jerked to a stop.

A circle of sirens and their axolotls grouped around them. Lenora recognized most of them as her new friends she'd met through Cetus, but no one came to her defense. Scowls and disgust greeted her.

Cetus was in front, smirking. He grew larger, his teeth extending in his mouth as Loxi made for the surface. Lenora kicked off his back.

Cetus intended to fight her, five to one. She couldn't believe she had once thought him a gentleman!

Panic flooded her brain. She'd only used her monstrous form the one time earlier today, and she didn't know how to fight or defend herself. How could she survive being this outnumbered by a group of well-trained sirens?

She bobbed into the open air, disoriented for a moment from the bright sunlight. A massive ship floated nearby in the waves, erasing her previous concerns. She swam toward it on the surface of the water.

"Get out of here! It isn't safe!" she screamed.

A man scrambled to the side, leaning over and looking down into the water. "Lenora!" Devonshire called. "It's you! It's really you! Hold on, I'll grab a rope."

"No, get out of here! The other sirens are here."

"I won't leave you again, Lenora. I love you. I came back to find you."

Her heart squeezed at his declaration, but before she could add her own confession, the ship lurched, swayed as if by an invisible current. Snakes of black spread over the surface of the water, as the horrific faces of sirens emerged. All five of her former friends roared into the open air.

Lenora tried to transform, but nothing happened. She could see Devonshire had secured his ears. Trembling, she closed her eyes and sang.

"Weary sirens
Let us bring you rest
Stop your toiling
Believe what is best

Relax, visit
In the ocean deep
Never striving
Lying down to sleep."

Her hair slithered from her scalp, and her body unfurled, stretching to its full size. Her mouth roared, filled again with dozens of rows of vicious teeth.

She feared what the captain would think of her now, but she had to keep him safe.

She leapt at Cetus, sending waves over the ship, but her rage had overtaken her so completely that her concern was a dull afterthought.

Her hair wrapped tendrils around Cetus's monstrous form, and she pulled him away from the ship. The sirens on either side of him approached her, while the other two went behind her. She flew above them with sodden, blue-feathered wings, nearly as large as the ship, while yanking Cetus through the surface of the water, secured in tendrils of her hair.

She needed to draw the other four sirens away from Devonshire and the ship. It looked as if her plan might work when harpoons struck the back of the closest creature.

The sirens turned to attack.

Lenora roared, gaining a moment of their attention while darting away with Cetus. But two of the monsters stayed back, making Lenora pause. She didn't want to leave Devonshire to his own devices.

She didn't get to make the choice, however, and her distraction cost her. One of the sirens sprang into the air, knocking her from the sky.

Howling in pain, Lenora crashed into the water. The monstrous noise she'd made sounded foreign to her own ears. A glance at the ship confirmed Devonshire and his new crew had defeated one of the sirens. She turned her attention to her attackers.

In the crash, Lenora had relaxed her grip on Cetus. He wriggled loose, and the three sirens closest to her widened their mouths, sucking in air.

Searing heat bubbled beneath her skin. Her resolve crumbled, replaced by gripping fear. The air rushing toward the sirens was coming from her. Her entire body weakened, like a husk being scooped out bit by horrible bit.

Loxi and Pearl smacked against one of the sirens, breaking his concentration. Lenora took the opening to go on the offense. Cetus's snaking hair aimed for her throat.

She dove into the water, but the black coils seized her, squeezing her neck and cutting off her breath. Her mouth widened against her will, and the horrible tugging sensation of the sirens feeding overtook her once more.

She blinked as a harpoon grazed Cetus, leaving a trail of red down his pale arm.

Devonshire.

The twisting of her insides subsided momentarily as Cetus and the two remaining sirens turned on the ship, leaving Lenora in her weakened state.

She told her mind to move, to attack, but she was a helpless observer. Her stomach twisted in painful knots, and her heart raced in a relentless pace, but the rest of her body was still. She floated through the water like a dead fish.

Shouting and terrible splashing made her body quiver, but she couldn't so much as lift a finger or a tendril of hair.

Within minutes, the three sirens capsized the ship.

Please, Maker, save Devonshire!

Cetus turned his attention back to her as the vessel sank into the water. She was helpless to help, helpless to fight. Her form flickered and shrank back to her regular size, and Lenora could move again.

She dove away from Cetus, kicking as fast as she could. She thought she'd managed to save herself when she was yanked back to the surface again.

Two of the sirens held her in place while Cetus opened his mouth wide.

Lenora saw another siren in the distance. She was even larger and more horrible than the rest of them.

It was her mother.

Lenora thought her mother had stayed back in her cavern, choosing the path of impartiality, but the furious roar and the slashing of her hair showed otherwise. She opened her mouth, wider than Lenora would've thought possible, and tore at the other sirens. She killed two of them almost instantly. Cetus shrank, trying to flee, but she wouldn't let him.

Lenora turned away, not wanting to see the rest.

Her heart sped up as she swam toward the overturned ship, praying Devonshire and his men had survived. Loxi swam toward her with the captain upon his back. He pulled off sodden bandages from around his ears.

"Captain!" she cried. "You're alright."

"Yes, thanks to you."

"You helped quite a bit as well… Why did you come back?"

He laughed. "You have to ask?"

"Yes, I do."

"I already told you, for you, Lenora. I love you." Dragging her to Loxi's side, he kissed her. It was every bit as electric as their earlier kiss, but she forced herself to pull away.

Lenora hadn't noticed her mother swim up behind them in her smaller form. "And what do you think of your fiancée now that you've seen her with her teeth?" Her tone dripped with accusation.

He smirked. "I'd better not cross her."

Lenora licked her lips, tasting the salt of the ocean. "You still want to marry me?"

"Yes, more than ever."

"To protect your ship?" Her mother cut in.

Devonshire shook his head. "Actually, that didn't seem to work very well the last time. Lenora can attest to that."

"We were attacked several times," Lenora explained, "but they never sank us, so I thought maybe I helped to keep us from sinking."

Her mother sighed. "No, they shouldn't have been able to attack you at all, Lenora. Guess the human side wins with that one." She narrowed her gaze on the captain, and Lenora wondered what criticisms she would offer, but her mother surprised her. "If you're still interested in my daughter, I give my blessing."

Lenora brought her hand to her mouth.

Devonshire looked into her eyes. "Thank you. I would like nothing more."

She leapt from Loxi to embrace her mother in the water. "Thank you for your blessing, and thank you for saving me. You should come with us."

Her mother's eyes sparkled with unshed tears. "No, Lenora. This is where I belong. I can't survive away from the ocean."

"But the others… Cetus's mother…"

She shrugged. "I may have to move, but I'll be fine. I'm a survivor."

Lenora nodded, her chest tightening. "Will I ever see you again?"

"I don't know, but if you come to the ocean, I promise to find you." Her mother's tears spilled over.

"Mother," Lenora cried, throwing her arms around her.

Her mother squeezed her back. "I can't tell you what it's meant to me to have you here. I'm glad you visited."

She laughed. "I am too, actually."

Her mother held her a long while before Lenora climbed on Loxi again and waved until her mother was little more than a dot bobbing in the distance.

Lenora turned to Devonshire. "Shouldn't we go find your crew? Are they alright?" She couldn't believe they'd forgotten them.

"There was no crew. I was the only one on that ship."

"How did you manage that?"

"With great difficulty, and I'm going to be in trouble. I borrowed that ship."

"From whom?"

"I don't know."

"So you stole it?"

"I told you I used to be a pirate."

They settled into comfortable silence as Loxi zipped along the surface, back to Oceanea.

Devonshire pointed behind them. They had a follower.

"Pearl, what're you doing here?"

In answer, Pearl swam up next to Loxi.

"I think they're together," Devonshire told her.

Lenora scoffed.

He pointed to Pearl. "Is she looking more blue-green to you?"

"What're you talking about?"

"I read a book about axolotls, after I found out you owned one. They change colors when they're pregnant."

"What?" She looked at the pair and laughed. "That's incredible!" She smacked her head. "I had no idea."

Loxi craned his neck, winking. She turned her attention back to the captain. "When did you have time for all this axolotl research, Captain?"

"Your father mentioned his daughter owned an axolotl. I thought it was interesting."

"It's odd to think that you knew about me before I knew about you. What else did he share with you?"

"Initially, I only knew you were part-siren, but once we made an arrangement, I bombarded him with questions." Devonshire chuckled. "He showed me your portrait and told me about your fiery temper, your love of finery, and your longing for adventure."

Her face heated. "And that didn't make you hesitate?"

"Not at all. I was smitten."

"Why did you keep your distance from me then?"

"I wanted to make sure we would come together on our own, not by force. I wouldn't go through with a marriage like that. You made your feelings clear that day at the ball…"

"I'm sorry. I didn't know you then."

"What about now?" His eyes glinted mischievously. "Would you say you know me now?"

She smiled. "I do."

Chapter Twenty-Six
Happily Ever After

It was early the next morning by the time they made it to shore. Lenora was thirsty and exhausted. She'd slipped off Loxi several times when she drifted off, only kept seated by Devonshire's vigilance.

The first rays of the sun glowed across the surface of the water, filling Lenora with warmth.

Home. She was finally home.

As they made it to the docks, she could make out a figure standing on the empty shore.

"Is that Father?" she asked.

Devonshire kissed her head. "I sent word to him before I left. I'd hoped I'd get you out, and he could meet us. Either way, I thought he should know."

"Thank you. You don't know what this means to me."

Loxi pulled up to the dock. Father yanked Lenora from his back with a strength she didn't know he possessed and held her in his arms.

"Please say you forgive me."

She paused. "I know you did what you thought was right, and you showed wisdom by selecting Devonshire, but you should've trusted me with the truth."

He squeezed her tighter. "You're right, Lenora, and I'm so sorry. I hope that you will forgive me. To think your mother harmed you…"

"She didn't. Not in the end. She protected me from the others. I think she was torn."

Father sniffled. "That's refreshing to hear."

Devonshire splashed out of the water behind them. "Do you have any drinking water for us?"

"Yes, back in the carriage."

They walked away before Lenora thought of her axolotl. She turned, intending to say goodbye, but the pair of salamanders were already scrambling after her on the wooden dock.

"You can shrink back down!" she gasped as she lifted them into her palm.

They nodded.

"Does that mean you both want to come with me?"

More nodding.

Father and Devonshire waited at the carriage.

Father told her, "I'll see if I can get a couple of tankards of water at the pub. All I brought were skins that they can't fit inside."

Lenora took a deep sip of the waterskin, leaning against Devonshire's shoulder.

The pair of axolotls smiled up at her, and she smiled back.

Devonshire kissed the top of her head, sliding his arm around her shoulder. "I know I've technically already asked, but would you marry me, Lenora?"

She looked up into his sun-weathered face and his deep brown eyes. "Nothing would make me happier."

***

Several days of rest later, Lenora set up a simple wedding. She didn't mind that the short notice would cut the numbers. She only wanted to marry her captain as quickly as possible.

Stretching in the bright morning light, she allowed Hettie to comb through her hair. She'd heard many complaints from her lady's maid about her tangled tresses and tanned skin, but Lenora was happy to be home.

"Have you tried on your mother's dress yet?"

"No." She smiled at her frowning maid. "I can tell it will fit. I wanted to save it for today."

Hettie tsked. "The ocean changed you. I can't understand why you won't at least have the tailor come…"

Lenora patted her hand, standing.

"I'm not done with your hair."

"I'd like to wear it down today, Hettie."

The maid gave an exasperated sputter before leaving the room. Lenora stared out of her window, remembering the last evening she'd spent at home, crying and waiting for Thomas McKraven.

Hettie had informed her that he'd broken off his engagement with Elisabeth and was courting another lady. She'd been surprised that the news only filled her with sympathy for her childhood friend.

A knock at her door made her straighten. She hoped Hettie wouldn't be back to pester her about her hair.

"Come in."

Father stepped into the room. "I wanted to see my daughter one last time before I have to give her away."

Lenora laughed. "We're only living a short distance from you, and you're welcome any time." Devonshire and Father had secured a family home, but they'd promised her she could visit the ocean.

"Still…" He squeezed her hand, and she pulled him into an embrace.

***

Father had the ballroom set up with hundreds of flowers despite Lenora insisting the ceremony could be simple. Devonshire waited next to the minister in the very spot she'd been engaged.

Lenora felt beautiful in her mother's dress – a lace white gown with a long train that reminded her of a tail, and of course, a pair of axolotls on her shoulder for the finishing touch.

As Father walked her slowly up to Devonshire, she heard a hoot of celebration. She turned, seeing the lined face of Percy in attendance among other startled Oceanean ladies and gentlemen.

Devonshire's eyes were glassy and warm. He extended his hand to her as the minister started, "We are gathered here today in the sight of the Maker."

A buzz ran through her body, making it hard to concentrate on anything but Devonshire. Loxi and Pearl scuttled about from shoulder to shoulder.

"Do you, William Devonshire, take thee Lenora Darlington to be your wife, as long as the ocean has its tide with a love as deep as the sea?"

"I do."

"And do you, Lenora Darlington, take thee William Devonshire to be your husband, honoring him as the captain of your heart and holding fast to him like a ship in the storms of life?"

"I do."

"I now pronounce you husband and wife. You may kiss your bride."

The captain dipped her before covering his mouth with her own. Her heart soared, and she thanked the Maker for his wisdom in guiding the two of them together.

The guests applauded, the axolotls danced, and Percy whooped.

The End

Courtney Denelsbeck

Thank you for reading!
*If you enjoyed this story, please leave a review on
Amazon and Goodreads and check out the other books
in the Realms of Lurin series and by this author.*

*Subscribe to Courtney's newsletter for an exclusive
Captain Devonshire POV prequel chapter!*

And They Lived
Happily Ever After

About the Author

When she's not stuck in magical worlds, Courtney is homeschooling her four daughters, chatting with her husband, drinking too much coffee, playing with her dog, or enjoying a Minnesota sunset. Before she wrote books, she designed baby toys and stuffed animals. She's always loved art and illustrates and designs her own books. Her focus is on creating immersive experiences that are whimsical and fun while weaving deeper themes and meaningful content throughout her stories. Her faith in Christ inspires and guides her content. Her debut novel, Red Fairy & Fox, released in 2024.

Please connect with her online for her newsletter, book updates, and exclusive content. If you enjoyed this book, please share a review on Amazon.
It helps more than you know!
Thank you!

NEWSLETTER &
WEBSITE SIGN-UP

Acknowledgments

Thank you to my fellow fantasy authors who contributed to the Realms of Lurin series, making my dream of a multi-author magical fantasy collaboration possible: Cara Ruegg, Maegwen Salley-Massie, Sofia Simpson, C.A. Meadows, Nellie Peters, Gabriella Batel, and Candice Pedraza Yamnitz.

Candice's amazing covers helped this series shine in the way it deserves.

Thank you to my proofreaders and editors for catching all my weird phrasing and typos: Lynn Pinyerd and Lindsay Fowler Galloway.

Several amazing beta readers took their own precious writing time to help me make this story better: Samatha Leigh, Ashley Evercott, Mary Saxer, Isabelle Knight, Maegwen Salley-Massie, and C.A. Meadows. Thank you again for your kind words, encouragement, and feedback. A special shoutout to C.A. Meadows for giving me the idea to use an axolotl in my story... It wouldn't have been the same without Loxi!!

Thank you to my family for supporting me and loving me.

I would also love to thank my readers and ARC team, without you, no one would know about this story!

AND most of all to Jesus Christ my Lord and Savior for forgiving me, seeing me, hearing me, and loving me, even though I don't deserve it.

Thanks for reading! Please add a short review on Amazon and Goodreads and let me know what you thought! Subscribe to my newsletter for a free bonus chapter from Captain Devonshire's POV, as well as other freebies, writing updates, and future book release information. Keep reading for a preview of *Morlave's School of Magic* and *Red Fairy & Fox.*

Connect with Courtney:

https://author-courtney-denelsbeck.mailerpage.io

denelsbeck.writes@gmail.com

INSTAGRAM.com/courtney.denelsbeck

FACEBOOK.com/AuthorCourtneyDenelsbeck

TikTok.com/@courtney.denelsbeck

X.com/denelsbeckwrite

Other Books in the Series

Realms of Lurin

A collection of standalone, magical, regency-inspired fantasy novellas

Sirens and Sea Captains by Courtney Denelsbeck

Petals and Poison by Cara Ruegg

Venom and Vows by Maegwen Salley-Massie

Fae and Flames by Sofia Simpson

Goblins and Crystals by C.A. Meadows

Witches and Wolves by Nellie Peters

Tempest and Tiger's Eye by Gabriella Batel

Beaux and Dragons by Candice Pedraza Yamnitz

Books by Courtney Denelsbeck

Fantasy Series:
RED FAIRY & FOX ADVENTURES
Xavier of the Northern Sea
(Short story prequel Newsletter subscriber exclusive)
Red Fairy & Fox
The Lonely Prince
The Great Destroyer

MORLAVE'S MAGICAL ADVENTURES
Morlave's School of Magic
Morlave's Quest for Magic
Morlave's Return to Magic
Morlave's Defense of Magic - late 2026 (Final Book!)

Standalone Fantasy books:
REALMS OF LURIN
Sirens and Sea Captains

The Circlet
A time-looping romantic fantasy standalone, late 2026

Morlave's School of Magic

Morlave's Magical Adventures, Book 1

"Congratulations! You are one of the gifted few selected to receive the coveted Yortsed Academy scholarship."

Cornelius Morlave long since accepted his fate to follow in his parents' footsteps, spending his days working in their modest shop. But when a letter with the distinctive wax crest arrives, everything changes. Morlave has been offered a full scholarship to Yortsed Academy, a prestigious school for magic.

As Morlave arrives at Yortsed, he struggles to perform even the most basic spells, convinced that he doesn't belong. But when he uncovers dangerous secrets, Morlave realizes that his destiny may lie within the walls of Yortsed Academy.

Filled with elves, orcs, and mysterious magic, Morlave's School of Magic is perfect for fans of *Harry Potter, Peter Jackson,* and *The Lord of the Rings*. This book will take you on a journey of friendship, danger, and first love through a medieval academy that will leave you wanting more.

Red Fairy & Fox

Red Fairy & Fox Adventures, Book 1

What happens when a talking fox leads you to a new world through a puddle?

Queen Red escapes her lavish, boring life and finds herself in a strange, barren world full of magical creatures. But when she is forced to accept her destiny, she must make a choice that will determine the fate of two kingdoms.

As she struggles to fulfill her newfound role as a hero, Red is constantly reminded of the threats facing her kingdom and the strain on its magic. But with the help of her snarky fox companion, she may just have a chance at saving her people.

Dive into the enchanting world of Red Fairy & Fox, a whimsical YA retelling of Alice in Wonderland. With its dual timelines, mysterious deaths, and portals to other worlds, this tale is perfect for fans of *the Chronicles of Narnia* and *the Wingfeather Saga.*